F
Fow

Fowler, Karen Joy.

The science of
herself.

CLARK PUBLIC LIBRARY

97

D1531652

Winner of the W
Shirley Ja ___ Award
Nebula Award
Commonwealth Award

"Unforgettable . . . incandescent . . . bewitching."
—*Los Angeles Times Book Review*

"Highly imaginative . . . In fine-edged and
discerning prose, [Fowler] manages to recreate both
life's extraordinary and its ordinary magic."
—*New York Times Book Review*

"Fowler's witty writing is a joy to read."
—*USA Today*

"An astonishing narrative voice, at once lyric
and ironic, satiric and nostalgic. . . . Fowler can
tell stories that engage and enchant."
—*San Francisco Chronicle*

CLARK PUBLIC LIBRARY
303 WESTFIELD AVENUE
CLARK, NJ 07066
732-388-5999

KAREN JOY FOWLER

PM PRESS OUTSPOKEN AUTHORS SERIES

The
Science
of Herself

plus...

The Science of Herself

plus

"The Motherhood Statement"

and

"The Pelican Bar"

and

"More Exuberant Than Is Strictly Tasteful"
Outspoken Interview

and

"The Further Adventures of the Invisible Man"

KAREN JOY FOWLER

PM PRESS | 2013

Clark Public Library-Clark, N.J.

F
Fow
3/25/14
u 3/29

Karen Joy Fowler © 2013
This edition © 2013 PM Press

Series editor: Terry Bisson

"The Pelican Bar" originally appeared in *Eclipse 3: New Science Fiction and Fantasy* (San Francisco: Night Shade Books, 2009).

"The Further Adventures of the Invisible Man" originally appeared in *Conjunctions 39: The New Wave Fabulists* (Annandale-on-Hudson, NY: Bard College, 2002).

ISBN: 978-1-60486-825-8
LCCN: 2013911521

10 9 8 7 6 5 4 3 2 1

PM Press
P.O. Box 23912
Oakland, CA 94623

Printed in the USA by the Employee Owners of Thomson-Shore in Dexter, Michigan
www.thomsonshore.com

Outsides: John Yates/Stealworks.com
Insides: Jonathan Rowland

Clark Public Library-Clark, N.J.

CONTENTS

THE SCIENCE OF HERSELF

*None but a woman can teach the science
of herself.*
—Jane Austen

IN 1814, ANNE ELLIOT came to Lyme Regis and watched
Louisa Musgrove fall from the steps of the breakwater
onto the rocks below. It was late November, so even
though the weather was good, the beach was empty of
bathers and bathing machines. To their left, they could
see the steep road spilling through the village, landing on
the expanse of level beach. It was, Austen tells us, a vista
both lovely and wonderful. The water was a dark Byronic
blue. Seagulls wheeled in the air above them, shrieking.
The air smelled of salt.

There might have been a scavenger or two, combing the tide-line for flotsam. Perhaps a fisherman had hauled his boat out, flipped it belly-up for repairs, and was hammering in the distance. Anne Elliot noticed none of these. Nor did she see a young girl, well known to the locals, selling snakestones, vertiberries, and devil's toenails from a stand. This girl might have identified the Elliot party as tourists, might have even been approaching them with a basket of curious rocks just in time to see Louisa fall.

Or not. Strangely dressed, lower class, odd in affect, and desperately poor, she was not really the kind of girl who wanders into an Austen novel.

•••

In 1803, Austen herself had come to Lyme Regis and met this same girl's father. His name was Richard Anning. He was a cabinetmaker. Austen needed some repair work done on the lid to a box; he was recommended to her. We know these things because she found the price he asked so offensively high that she noted it in her diary.

Not noted: Richard Anning was a dissenter from the Church of England, a Congregationalist, and an outlier even there, an activist who'd organized a protest over the food shortages occasioned by the Napoleonic Wars and worked with the dominant church on issues of Poor Law.

Also not noted: his second career. Richard Anning was a fossil hunter. There is no mention of fossils in Austen's descriptions of the charms of Lyme Regis, yet it was said that smugglers could identify the beach in the dark simply by raking with their fingers through the sand. Two hundred million years ago, Lyme Regis lay at the bottom of a tropical sea, but no one knew this yet or would have believed it if they had.

Austen came again the following year. She and her sister Cassandra were uncommonly hardy, continuing their ocean bathing long into October. In 1804, they witnessed together the great fire that destroyed some fifty houses in Lyme.

Five years after Austen's second visit and five years before Anne's, Richard Anning died. He left behind a wife, two living children—a son, Joseph, thirteen at the time, and a daughter, Mary, ten—and eight dead and in the graveyard. Also a debt of £120. Within a year, the family was on parish relief.

• • •

Lyme's most notable manmade feature is the Cobb, the large wall of stone that curves around the harbor and has done so since at least 1328. The day they arrived, the Elliot party walked on top of the Cobb until they tired of the wind, and then descended to its shelter by a particularly steep set of stairs known as Granny's Teeth. They talked of poetry and ships, war and a young curate's prospects.

They stayed in Lyme only one night. Many of the inns and boarding houses, the indoor baths and the Assembly Rooms were closed. In the summer, they might have gone into the sea, a bell ringing to warn men to stay away as the ladies bathed. In November, Lyme had dwindled to its actual residents. Winter was the wrong season for tourists.

Winter was the season for fossil hunting. Ninety-five miles of crumbling cliffs stretch like wings on either side of Lyme Regis. These cliffs contain shale, lime, and sandstone in an unstable proportion particular to Lyme and called the Blue Lias. In the winter, storms strip and shift the terrain, exposing new bits of cliff face, tumbling old bits back into the sea. A fossil can appear after one storm, scrubbed free by the wind and rain, only to disappear again after the next. Diligence and persistence are required, but also courage. There can be no waiting for the weather to clear, no waiting for the tides to recede. The fossil hunter must wade and climb. Landslips are common, the waves treacherous.

The chief peril is the hanging cliffs. At any moment they may give, crushing anyone underneath. Later in her life, Mary Anning's beloved dog Tray was killed in just this way only a few feet from where she stood. Richard Anning was often criticized for taking his children into this dangerous terrain; he did so even on the Lord's Day. He himself had at least one serious fall and the resulting injuries usually share the blame with tuberculosis for his early death.

That young Joseph and Mary continued this work without him—that their mother, who had already lost so many of her children, allowed it—shows how desperate their finances were. Mary made her first sale in the period just after her father died. A Londoner gave her half a crown for a very fine ammonite, enough to feed them for a week. She was eleven years old.

Sometime later that same year, her older brother Joseph found a massive ichthyosaurus skull in a fallen rock. The skull measured almost four feet from snout to neck. He called Mary to come and see and they knelt together in the whipping wind and rain. The sockets of its eyes were twelve inches across.

The children were used to not knowing what it was that they had found. Ammonites were called snakestones because people thought they might be petrified snakes. Belemnites were caused by lightning and known therefore as thunderbolts. The world was vast and mysterious and no one knew how it was about to tip over.

But Mary had never seen a fossil so big as this one. What did she think as she looked into the eye sockets of that enormous skull? Did she suddenly wonder if the bay was still hiding other such beasts, beasts alive and hunting? That when she waded in the tidewaters, searching for her stones, those enormous, predatory eyes were watching her legs? Or did she already know more than enough about monsters—her life so hard, her heart so full of grief? She had been very close to her father.

Did she see only the money such an object would bring?

We do know what Joseph thought. He thought that fossil hunting was not for him and from then on he mostly left it to his little sister. He apprenticed as an upholsterer, trading any present income for future earnings. By the time those occurred, he would be married with a child of his own.

A mudslide buried the skull before it could be moved, the creature having raised its enormous head only briefly and then returned to the deep. Tides and storms prevented further searching for almost a year, and it was Mary, aged twelve now, who finally found it again, and also the rest of the skeleton in the cliffs high above.

The event was reported in a local newspaper:

> A few days ago, immediately after the late high tide, was discovered, under the cliffs between Lyme Regis and Charmouth, the complete petrifaction of a crocodile, 17 feet in length, in a very perfect state.

This was the first ichthyosaurus ever to be found so complete. The Annings sold it to Henry Hoste Henley, the lord of the manor of Colway. Henley was also their landlord; no competitive bids were entertained. They got £23 for the specimen minus the wages of the workmen who dug it out.

Henley sold it in turn to a collector named William Bullock, and Bullock exhibited it in his Museum of Natural Curiosities in Piccadilly. In 1814, Everard Home, a surgeon and recent Baronet, wrote the first of six papers, all riddled with errors, arguing that the creature's anatomy suggested a closer relationship to fish than to crocodiles. It had a fish's delicate spine, four fin-shaped limbs, and a fish's tail. But the plates in its eyes were more like a bird's. In short, no one had ever seen a creature like it. It remained a mystery that opened into more mysteries, an infinite, unsettling puzzle box. What world did we live in? Whose world did we live in?

In 1819, it was sold again, in auction to Charles Konig of the British Museum, as a "crocodile in a fossil state." Konig was the first to suggest the name ichthyosaurus or fish lizard.

More papers were written and delivered and debated. Over in France, Georges Cuvier was gaining support for his extinction theory. His research, he said, seemed to prove the existence of a world previous to ours, destroyed by some catastrophe. But many scientists still hoped for an explanation in keeping with biblical dogma. The catastrophe could well have been the biblical flood, except that the animals had all been saved, two by two by two. God would never be so profligate, so wasteful as to make a creature only to lose its kind entirely. The theory of extinction suggested mistakes, or at the very least divine inattention. The church responded to each new theory with increasing alarm.

In any case, these perplexing matters were now comfortably in the hands of rich, and often titled, men. The price of Mary's specimen had risen to £45, and her role in recovering and cleaning it had already been forgotten by everyone outside Lyme Regis.

• • •

She was the second Anning girl to be named Mary. The first had died at the age of four, when, her mother having left the room for only a minute, she'd tried to add wood chips to the fire and her clothes had caught. It was Christmastime.

Five months later, her mother gave birth to the second Mary and this Mary also had a perilous childhood. The Annings lived so close to the water that the house often flooded. On one occasion the family had to climb out through an upstairs window to avoid being drowned in their own kitchen.

On another, a family friend, a woman named Elizabeth Haskings, took the baby Mary to nearby Rack Field for a show of horsemanship. The riders wheeled and danced their horses. They wore red vests and red ribbons were threaded through the horses' manes. Half the town had turned out to see them.

Mary lay against Elizabeth, her breath on Elizabeth's neck, one hand clutching her collar. Mary was small for her age, limp in Elizabeth's arms, and damp with her own heat. A wind came up and Elizabeth moved to the shelter of a nearby elm. The hooves of the horses pounded on the dirt like thunder. The sky opened white and struck, lightning without rain. Elizabeth Haskings was killed instantly along with two fifteen-year-old girls, friends from the village. John Haskings, Elizabeth's widower, wrote later, "The Child was taken from my wifes arms and carried to its parents in appearance dead but they was advised to put it in warm water and by so doing it soon recovered."

The crowd at Rack Field had followed to the Annings' house and waited outside. When the physician came to tell them that the baby had survived, *a miracle*, he said, the cheering could be heard even over the sound of the surf, all the way down to the Cobb.

Decades later, her nephew wrote that Mary had been born a sickly, listless child, but the lightning bolt turned her bright and lively. Perhaps there was simply no other way to explain a woman of her class and time, intelligent but little educated, no money, and an outcast Dissenter, who taught herself French so as to read Cuvier, followed the shifting theories of pre-Darwinian science with acuity, and had her own ideas about the objects she had found, touched, pried from the rocks, cleaned and polished for presentation. Like the fossils, she defied explanation.

• • •

Mary had begun fossil hunting at the age of five. She'd followed her father so tenaciously among the cliffs that he'd made a pick and hammer especially for her, something to fit her little hands. Back in his workroom, he taught her to chip away the rock, and then to clean and polish the fossil that emerged. Sometimes the work was so delicate it had to be done with a sewing needle. Her father teased her that she was, like any other girl, learning her needlework.

After his death, she roamed the beaches in her odd get-up—filthy clogs, multiple tattered skirts, one on top of the next for warmth, and then a patched cloak flung over the whole. She wore a man's top hat, stuffed with paper and shellacked for protection from falling rocks. Quite thin, but seen from a distance, kitted out for fossil hunting, she resembled a small round hut with a hat for a chimney.

She was not always alone on the beach. In 1812, someone new came to Lyme, a boy with prospects, sixteen years old to Mary's thirteen, and, like Tom Bertram in *Mansfield Park*, heir to a sugar plantation in Jamaica. Austen would have seen the possibilities. The only sure way out of poverty for Mary was to marry up.

She might have been more marriageable if she hadn't made a habit of picking up creatures that washed ashore and dissecting them on the Anning kitchen table. She was not a pretty girl and she had no pretty ways.

The boy's name was Henry De la Beche. Recently booted from military school for insubordination, he'd come to join his mother and her third husband at their home on Broad Street. There is no record of how he and Mary met, but we can imagine it as Austen might have written it—the older boy, in disgrace, but with the confidence of wealth, education, and good looks. Then Mary, who should have been quiet and deferential in his company, but was not.

At thirteen, she was already the expert on the Blue Lias. People talked later of how sharp her eye was, how she would set her chisel into the cliff at some spot no different from any other spot and, after a few blows, reveal the small skeleton of an ancient fish. If it was fossils Henry wanted, he did best to listen to her, keep in her good graces.

He did want fossils. He was as keen on fossils as a boy could be, given that he didn't need to find them in order to eat. Soon after meeting Mary, he had decided on a career in geology. They were often seen scouring the cliffs after a storm, their heads bent together over some find, their hands touching accidentally as they worked a specimen free. Mary's fingers would be rough and scraped, her nose red from the wind and salt. Mr. Elliot, Anne's father, would have been the first to note that she was seldom out in such weather as would improve her looks.

Sometimes an older woman, Miss Elizabeth Philpot, a noted collector who also lived in Lyme, joined them. But often it was just the two of them, alone in the wind and the water, scrambling about the cliffs.

He did not marry her. At twenty-one, he came into his fortune and used it to travel to sites of geological interest, to meet prominent scholars in the field. He was able, as she was not, to join the prestigious Geological Society of London. He was writing papers by then; one entitled "Memoir on the Genus Ichthyosaurus" consisted mostly of descriptions of Mary's finds.

Mary had continued to uncover skeletons. These, varying greatly in size and with subtle differences, particularly in regard to their teeth, suggested four distinct subspecies of ichthyosaurus. She learned of his marriage to the beautiful Letitia Whyte only after it had occurred. They continued as good friends, the carpenter's daughter and the plantation owner's son, although he was much less often in Lyme now.

By then she had other partners. Her terrier, Tray. Elizabeth Philpot on many occasions. And, when she was only sixteen, an Oxford professor named William Buckland. He had written to her first, asking for the privilege of accompanying her on her hunts. Buckland was a noted eccentric, a jokester, whose rooms at Oxford were filled with birds and mice, guinea pigs, snakes, and frogs. As a young man, he'd vowed to eat his way through the animal kingdom and was infamous for serving mice on toast to unsuspecting guests. The bluebottle fly, he said, was the worst-tasting animal he'd found.

Other geologists—the Anglican clergyman, William Conybeare, and Jean-André De Luc—came often to Lyme Regis during these same years and these men sought Mary out, young and poor as she was. She listened to them and they to her. She grew accustomed to the company of her betters. The residents of Lyme noticed.

These guests sometimes brought her papers from the various scientific societies. Mary copied these out, including the drawings, which she did very deftly. She read well and had a good hand. She deeply regretted not being able to go to the museums in London to see what could be seen.

She noticed that the men who'd bought the fossils from her were being credited with finding them. In addition to thinking well of herself, she began to feel hard done by. For all the flattering attention, her family's finances had not improved.

At thirteen, a neighbor had given her a book on geology, the first book she'd ever owned, and over the subsequent years, she had read it to tatters, carried on with her dissections, and learned to make her careful drawings, her beautiful, detailed descriptions of the fossils she found. She was becoming impressively learned. She was every inch a scientist.

• • •

She was a complete romantic. Fond of poetry, her fourth commonplace book (the first through third are lost) began with Lord Byron's "January 22nd, Missolonghi" copied onto the page.

'Tis time this heart should be unmoved,
    Since others it has ceased to move;
Yet though I cannot be beloved,
    Still let me love.

Though perhaps she chose this poem not for the rejected melancholy of its opening verses but for its later impulse toward glorious self-sacrifice. Anna Maria Pinney, a wealthy sixteen-year-old who met Mary when Mary was in her thirties and was clearly dazzled, wrote in her diary, "Had she lived in an age of chivalry she might have been a heroine with fearless courage, ardour, and peerless truth and honour."

Awake! (not Greece—she *is* awake!)
    Awake, my Spirit! Think through *whom*
Thy life-blood tracks its parent lake
    And then strike home!

• • •

One morning, Mary was out early, the remnants of the storm still gusting about her, stinging her cheeks with salt. The year was 1815. The Napoleonic Wars would soon see their final battle. Anne Elliot was off somewhere, enjoying her happy ending.

Something large had washed up on the Lyme beach. Smugglers' brandy often came ashore. Mary usually hid any contraband she found until it could be quietly retrieved. Lyme looked after Lyme and not the excise men. But this was not a box. She approached it cautiously. Perhaps she was finally to see one of her crocodiles in the flesh. Perhaps it was only a seal.

What she found was the body of a woman, lying with her face to the sky, her long hair tangled with seaweed, her eyes open and milky. Her sodden clothes were beautifully and expensively made.

Mary knelt and cleaned the sand from her face, untangled the seaweed from her hair, pulled her skirts so that her legs were covered. The woman was still beautiful, and Mary immediately associated her with Ophelia or some other storied creature. There was something so intimate in her ministrations as to make her feel that she had known this woman. The finding and the loss of her seemed like the exact same thing since they had happened at the exact same moment.

She saw the body taken into the church and then went there daily, to pray over her and to bring fresh flowers. As long as the woman went unidentified there was no one she belonged to more than Mary. Mary invented many pasts for her, many ways she might have ended on the beach. Tragic love stories, desperate gestures.

Eventually she was identified as a Lady Jackson, lost in the wreck of the *Alexander* with her husband and children. The *Alexander*, inbound from Bombay, had gone down in a gale on Easter Monday in a part of Chesil Beach known as Deadman's Cove. There were only five survivors, none of whom spoke English, and no account of the ship's final hours, so close to home after a journey of 155 days, has survived. Friends came from London to take charge and Mary felt the loss not just of the body but of the stories she had told herself about the body. No Lady Jackson had been listed on the ship's manifest. There remained just that bit of mystery.

Fifteen years later, Mary recounted this to Anna Maria Pinney. Mary had been just sixteen when she found Lady Jackson. Pinney was just sixteen when Mary told her about it. The romance may well have doubled in the double adolescent telling of it. Anne Elliot would have recommended less poetry in the diet and more prose to the both of them.

• • •

When she was nineteen, Mary met Lieutenant Colonel Thomas James Birch, a retired officer of fifty-two, comfortably well off and a great collector of fossils. He began visiting Lyme, calling on Mary and her mother and usually making several purchases.

On one such occasion, he found both Mary and her mother in tears. He made them sit, brought cups of tea. He feared something dreadful had happened to Joseph, but the problems turned out to be financial. After years of support, there was to be no more money from the parish. Mary had not found a valuable fossil for many months. "We are selling the furniture," Mary's mother told him. There was little enough of it, but all made by her dead husband. "And once that's gone, we've no rent, we've no roof over our heads."

Birch's sympathies were aroused, but also his anger. As valuable as Mary's contributions to science had been, it wasn't right that the Annings should be facing eviction. He would not have it.

He put the whole of his own collection up for auction, 102 items in all, an extraordinary grouping that he had gathered over years and continents. Many of these were things that Mary had found. The sale created enormous excitement. It lasted three days and drew bidders from Germany, France, Austria, and, of course, England. Cuvier himself bought several pieces. When it was over, Birch had earned more than £400, all of which he gave to the Anning family. For the first time in their lives, the Annings were financially secure.

The auction had also drawn a great deal of attention to Mary. Most of it was scientific. That such a young girl was capable of the arduous, dangerous work of fossil collecting! That she had found so many exemplary specimens!

Some of it was romantic. What had possessed Birch to make such an astonishing gesture? Rumors arose about the young girl and the old man; it was whispered that she *attended* to him on his visits to Lyme. Fortunately, according to Pinney's diaries, Mary "glories in being afraid of no one." She went out and bought herself a bonnet, though as a Dissenter it cannot have been a gaudy one.

• • •

Three years later, Mary made her greatest find. She was out on a particularly treacherous section of cliff known as the Black Ven when she saw something, some bit of shine, still mostly covered with shale. It was December, the day after a great storm, and she was working in a blustery wind with an intermittent icy spray of rain. She spent all morning, chipping away the slate, her fingers numb and stiff with cold. When she was done, she had a skull unlike any she had ever seen.

She left her dog Tray to guard the spot and called on men from the village to help her before the tide returned. They worked into the evening until the whole skeleton had been revealed, nine feet long and six feet wide, but with a strangely elongated neck and a strangely tiny head. The creature had paddles instead of feet and would have resembled a turtle if not for the neck.

Conybeare had speculated on the possibility of this creature from fragments he'd found and now here was the whole of it. He responded with jubilation, writing to Henry De la Beche who was off in Jamaica attending his plantation. "The Annings have discovered an entire Plesiosaurus," Conybeare wrote. Mary had made meticulous drawings of the skeleton and one of these went to Henry, her childhood friend.

Another found its way to Georges Cuvier. Cuvier said that the neck was far too long—thirty-five vertebrae—when no creature that walked on four legs had more than seven. Birds might have as many as twenty-five, reptiles no more than eight, and this was clearly a reptile. Mary, he suggested, had taken the head of a snake and put it on the body of an ichthyosaur. He felt he could even identify the place in the neck where she had made the joining.

Skeletons in the Blue Lias were often found scattered; there was always the danger of mistakenly welding two creatures together. But Cuvier was not alleging a mistake. He was accusing Mary of deliberate fraud.

A special meeting of the Geological Society of London was called, which, as a woman, Mary could not have attended even if she'd had the money to go to London. She paced the beach at dawn, prayed in the church at noon, picked at her dinner as she waited to hear. Sleep was impossible. She was still so young. The wrong finding would destroy her reputation and end her career.

The skeleton had been shipped by sea to London but didn't arrive in time, and Mary's drawings had to suffice. The meeting went late, hot with debate, a duel of science against science. Around this same time, Mary wrote a letter, which contained the following: "The world has used me so unkindly, I fear it has made me suspicious of all mankind."

By the end of the meeting, Cuvier had completely recanted. On closer inspection, he accepted Mary's specimen as the genuine article.

The village of Lyme Regis did not fare as well; the year ended in an epic storm. The first floor of the Annings' house flooded and all their fossils had to be moved to the upstairs, where Tray whimpered and the family huddled as the wind howled outside. Dozens of ships along the coast went down, scores of people drowned. Trees were pulled from the ground and hurled down the hills. The great Cobb itself cracked and let the ocean through.

• • •

Mary had at least two close friendships with younger women. Both were diarists; both are remembered only because they left a record of her. Both appear to have been thoroughly infatuated, at least initially. Frances Augustus Bell was the first of these. Sickly herself, she was greatly impressed with Mary's strength and courage. On one occasion, out on the cliffs with a dangerous tide already at their ankles, she says that Mary simply seized her and carried her up the cliffs to safety. She describes Mary as a person impossible to dislike.

But Anna Maria Pinney, who knew Mary later and wrote more of her, said that she "gossiped and abused almost everyone in Lyme" and that the company of her own class had become distasteful to her. Her likes and her dislikes, Pinney said, were equally violent and unshakeable.

Visitors to Lyme vary greatly in their descriptions of her over the years:

"A clever funny Creature."

"A prim, pedantic, vinegar-looking, thin female, shrewd and rather satirical in her conversation."

"A strong, energetic spinster of about twenty-eight years [she would have been thirty-eight at this time] . . . *tanned and masculine in expression . . ."*

"She would serve us with the sweetest temper, bearing with all our little fancies and never finding us too trouble-some as we turned over her trays of curiosities."

"It is certainly a wonderful instance of divine fa-vour—that this poor, ignorant girl . . . understands more of the science than anyone else in this kingdom."

By the time she was twenty-seven, Mary had saved enough money to buy a shop with a glass display window in the front. She named it Anning's Fossil Depot and she and her mother lived in the rooms above. In 1844, King Frederick Augustus II of Saxony visited her there and for £15 purchased an entire ichthyosaurus skeleton. His physician who accompanied him wrote the following:

> We had alighted from the carriage and were proceeding on foot, when we fell in with a shop in which the most remark-able petrifications and fossil remains—the head of an *Ichthyosaurus*, beautiful ammo-nites, etc.—were exhibited in the window. We entered and found the small shop and adjoining chamber completely filled with fossil productions of the coast . . .

He asked Mary Anning for her name and address which she wrote in his notebook. "I am well known throughout the whole of Europe," she told him since he seemed not to know this already.

•••

In 1833, an entry in Anna Maria Pinney's diary alludes to a deep sorrow, given in strictest confidence and too delicate to set down in its details. Whatever it was, Pinney kept the secret, noting only that eight years earlier Mary had hoped to see herself raised from her low situation and had seen those hopes cruelly dashed.

The world dislikes a story in which a woman is merely accomplished, brave, and consequential. Eight years before, Letitia De la Beche had sought a legal separation from Henry alleging ill treatment, which may have simply been his long years without her in Jamaica. A year later, she'd taken up residence with her lover, Major General Wyndham. We've no reason beyond the faint hint of Pinney's diary to believe that Mary wanted Henry. If she did, like Anne Elliot, she'd had this second chance. But Henry took off for the continent to escape the scandal and Mary found a pterosaur, the first in England, instead.

•••

In 1830, Henry came to Mary with an offering. He had painted a watercolor for her entitled "Duria Antiquior, A More Ancient Dorset." This crowded Jurassic landscape, largely underwater, included every creature Mary had found, and most of them trying to eat each other. It was an astonishing act of imagination, beautifully rendered.

But it was not the painting that was Henry's chief gift. Mary had lost her money in a bad investment; the market for fossils had slowed, and once again her finances were precarious. Lithographic prints had been made from Henry's painting and were being briskly sold. All the proceeds were to be Mary's. Henry hoped her fossil sales would be boosted as well by the advertising.

Meanwhile her old friend William Buckland persuaded the British Association for the Advancement of Science to grant her an annuity of £25 a year. No other woman had ever been half so acknowledged. When secured, it was enough to keep her and her mother, too, even if she never made another great find.

• • •

A decade passed and a few years more. Mary Anning continued to uncover fossils—ichthyosaurs, plesiosaurs, and pterosaurs, but also the *Squaloraja polyspondyla*, the fish *Dapedius,* the shark *Hybodus.* In 1839, she wrote a letter to the *Magazine of Natural History*, part of which was published. She was correcting a claim made in one of their articles, that a recent *Hybodus* fossil was the first of its kind, a new genus, since she had already discovered several others. She was among the earliest to recognize coprolites for what they were—petrified feces—and sold sketches made from the ink she discovered still in the ink sacs of belemnite fossils.

She narrowly escaped a drowning. She was nearly crushed by a runaway carriage. She was only a few feet away from the cliff collapse that killed her Tray, her constant companion.

Prominent scientists such as Louis Agassiz and Richard Owen continued to seek her out, to, in Owen's words, "take a run down to make love to Mary Anning at Lyme." Owen routinely omitted her role when discussing her finds, but in the early 1840s, Agassiz named two fish fossils for her—*Acrodus anningiae* and *Belenostomus anningiae*. He was the only person to so acknowledge her while she was still alive to enjoy it. He even threw in *Eugnathus philpotae*, for her good friend, the collector, Elizabeth Philpot. Both women had impressed him enormously.

Mary was part now of the great debates, even if only from the counter of her fossil shop. The theory of catastrophism waned in favor of uniformitarianism, geological change coming slowly and uniformly rather than in a series of catastrophes. Biblical stories fell beneath Agassiz's glaciers and Lyell's recurring cycles of climate change. Darwin was about to speak.

Henry De la Beche was named director of the British Geological Survey. As such he was more interested in finding the materials to fuel the British Empire—tin, iron, and coal—than in fossils. William Buckland was named dean of Westminster, and occupied with problems of cholera and sewage. Lyme was hit, first with disastrous landslips that caused whole houses to fall from the cliffs, and then with fire. Mary lost her dog and then her mother. She found a lump in one of her breasts.

• • •

These things Mary Anning and Jane Austen shared: that they made their own way in the world, and that they are remembered. Tourists come to Lyme to see the inn where Austen stayed or the place where Mary Anning's shop once stood, and some, like Lord Tennyson, come to see the exact spot where Louisa Musgrove fell. They shared this, too, that they both died young: Austen at forty-one and Mary at forty-seven.

Austen's death came in 1817, the same year Mary's first ichthyosaurus was named, the same year *Persuasion* was published. Austen had worked on Anne's story until illness prevented her and would have worked on it more had she been able. Its publication was posthumous.

Mary Anning made it into Jules Verne's books in the guise of her monsters, but never into Austen's. She wouldn't have made sense there with her bits of gothic history, her lightning, her science, her creatures. She wouldn't make sense in any story until the story changed.

• • •

Austen's story does not.

Anne Elliot is standing in the shelter of the Cobb, her cloak pulled tightly around her. The seagulls float above on currents, glide with their wings outstretched through the air. The day is cloudless, but the sun is thin. Anne is certain that Captain Wentworth no longer loves her and yet, Austen tells us, she is coming into a second bloom. She has recently been admired by a young man in passing who will propose to her before the story's end. All Anne has to do to see young Mary approaching in her curious clothes with her curious rocks is turn.

But the moment is already past. Austen is tired; she is dying. Her pen moves and Anne's mouth opens in fear and horror. Into the charming setting of Lyme Regis, just as Austen remembers it from her visits long ago, Louisa Musgrove falls.

THE MOTHERHOOD STATEMENT

The "Turkey City Lexicon," a primer for science fiction workshops, currently contains the following:

The Motherhood Statement

SF story which posits some profoundly unsettling threat to the human condition, explores the implications briefly, then hastily retreats to affirm the conventional social and humanistic pieties, e.g. apple pie and motherhood. Greg Egan once stated that the secret of truly effective SF was to deliberately "burn the motherhood statement."

As general advice, I have no problem with this. Easy assumptions should always be examined and examined again. The coinage is catchy and rolls off the tongue. Something important is being said.

It's the specifics that give me pause. Apple pie, okay, fine, whatever. But motherhood? Nothing, absolutely nothing, appears to me more contested in our political and social and private lives than motherhood. Any woman who has ever had children can tell you it is no picnic of affirmation. Any woman who has not had children can tell you that that, too, is a controversial place to be. Neither is much admired.

Motherhood is a concept that changes from culture to culture and over time. Sometimes, it's set in opposition to mothering—motherhood, in this schematic, is the sacred duty of women, an artificial construct which underlies the whole system of patriarchy. In this system, a woman with no children is a shirker. Mothering, on the other hand, is simply the work of first bearing and then raising a child. The biological mother need not be the same person who raises the child. The person (or people) who raises the child need not be female. The extent to which this second formulation, mothering, can be untangled from any imposed societal values is unclear. (At the very least, the untangling would be the work of generations.)

Childcare has too often been, as Adrienne Rich once noted, a form of enforced servitude or a duty performed out of guilt with its own unhappy consequences.

Equally problematic is the argument that mothers, or women in general, have a particular gift for nurturance and that by putting our politics into the hands of women this gift will transform the world.

Not that the world doesn't desperately need transforming.

While doing primate research for my most recent novel, I read many pages about Harry Harlow's infamous studies of rhesus monkey infants raised with replacement mothers, inanimate mothers made of cloth or wire. It's important to remember that these experiments took place against a backdrop of considerable scientific hostility toward mothers. "Mother love is a dangerous instrument," John B. Watson, president of the American Psychological Association had said with considerable impact. The influence of the mother should be limited as much as possible and eventually, in some utopian future, eliminated altogether. The "overkissed child" was debilitated for life by such unnecessary affections.

But here is what we think we now know: love (often, but not always mother love) changes the young brain and those changes have permanent consequences. Neuroplasticity is the necessary ability of the brain to rearrange itself, and love is neuroplasticity's primary source.

A subsequent movement, often exemplified by Dr. Benjamin Spock, assured mothers that they knew more than they thought they knew and encouraged them to trust themselves above all. Affection was okay again; in fact it was essential. World War II had shown us infants who died without it.

According to some, Spock's advice created an American generation, the baby-boomers of the 1960s, which is a good thing or not, depending on how you think. As one of them, I can attest to the fact that we have never been popular. But we have, some of us, been happy.

Freud, Skinner, and Bettelheim all took their shot at mothers. For many years Bettelheim blamed bad mothering for autism. Our current vocabulary includes "the helicopter mother," "the tiger mother," and "the good-enough mother." Also postpartum depression and the murderous mother.

So which motherhood statement are we burning today?

• • •

You will have noted that all the authorities I've quoted so far are male. But since the early 1900s at least, women's literatures have been fighting over the societal and personal issues raised by actual or anticipated reproductive technologies. I started reading science fiction in the 1970s and quickly found my way to the great women writing at that time. I was so thoroughly imprinted by these foundational reading experiences that it took me quite some time to notice that the field of science fiction was not dominated by women.

Nevertheless, during these years, the great science fiction writers were busily burning the motherhood statement. They imagined worlds in which babies were birthed by machines; worlds in which reproduction occurred through cloning or parthenogenesis or with extraterrestrial participation. They pictured motherhood as a paying job or else as a shared responsibility. In Susy McKee Charnas's *Motherlines*, every child has five mothers. They imagined worlds in which women were forcibly impregnated and incarcerated in birthing rooms, or worlds in which women freely chose the fathers of their children from sperm banks. They imagined pregnant men. They imagined worlds, like Ursula Le Guin's *The Left Hand of Darkness*, in which sexuality is so fluid that the same person might be the biological father of one child and the biological mother of another, or worlds like Vonda McIntyre's "Dreamsnake," in which birth control is a biological function that can be learned rather than a right that one must continually fight to keep. The imagining of separatist, all-women worlds often foundered on the issue of sons. It was apparently all too possible to imagine women giving up their fathers and their husbands. Considerable tap-dancing must happen in order to imagine that mothers will give up their sons. At the same time many of these writers and others spoke openly about the anger mothers often feel at the daily abnegation of self that motherhood demands, the impossible requirements of the job.

Much has been written about cyberpunk and its bodily modifications, its transcendence of the physical.

The cyberpunks had much less interest in the body, especially in the bodily issues of reproduction than the feminists who preceded them. In that way, they represented a return to the more usual mode of genre literatures, the mode in which mothers hardly appear at all. One could argue, I'm sure, that the erasure of the whole topic of motherhood from a literature would qualify as burning the motherhood statement. But not in a very interesting way.

In fact, since the 1970s and '80s, there has never again been in the field such a concentrated and communal attempt to reimagine motherhood. The texts of the second-wave feminists are sometimes seen as outdated partly by their focus on these very issues.

But fast forward to the present. I know of at least one case where an editor (who eventually did take the story in question) worried about publishing a piece in which a fictional woman got a fictional abortion. In the United States, 624 bills regulating women's bodies have already been passed and the year is only half over. Ohio has gutted women's reproductive rights as part of their budget and Wisconsin has done the same. Texas is taking their second run at it and, unless Wendy Davis can filibuster for thirty more hours, will soon follow suit. And these are just the most recent states to do so. Don't even ask about Kansas. Never ask about Kansas.

I can remember no other time in which the attacks on women's freedom have been so widespread, so sustained, and so successful. Or half so scary. Incest and

rape exceptions are now routinely contested and eliminated by legislation; when the forced-birth movement is
finished, even the life of the mother will be insufficient
grounds for a legal abortion. An argument that begins
by positing women valuable only as mothers will end by
suggesting that, even as mothers, women are not valuable
at all.

Meanwhile the assault has moved unapologetically
from abortion to birth control. A sizable chunk of the
population has shown themselves to be absolutely com-
mitted to forcing motherhood upon women as the price
for having sex. Under these circumstances, motherhood
becomes a mechanism for controlling the lives of and
limiting the possibilities for women, often openly and
consciously so.

In 1976, Adrienne Rich wrote, "We need to imagine a world in which every woman is the presiding genius
of her own body. In such a world . . . sexuality, politics,
intelligence, power, motherhood, work, community, in-
timacy, will develop new meanings; thinking itself will be
transformed. This is where we have to begin."

This is where we have to begin again and with
urgency.

Motherhood is an issue crucially impacted by
class, race, and culture, and must be recognized as such.
Simultaneously, it is the first principle and the thing
that we all still, at least as of 2013, share—that we all
had mothers. Who mothered or didn't mother us and
what support or condemnation the surrounding society

provided to them still matters in the deepest possible way to our personal lives and to society as a whole. One cannot truly imagine the future without addressing the issue.

The easy assumption that motherhood constitutes some easy assumption is neither accurate nor serving us well. Go ahead and burn it, whatever you think it is. I'm all in favor. We needed a new motherhood statement anyway. It would be so great if, after the burning, you helped with that, too.

THE PELICAN BAR

FOR HER BIRTHDAY, NORAH got a Pink CD from the twins, a book about vampires from her grown-up sister, *High School Musical 2* from her grandma (which Norah might have liked if she'd been turning ten instead of fifteen), an iPod shuffle plus an Ecko Red T-shirt and two-hundred-dollar darkwash Seven Jeans—the most expensive clothes Norah had ever owned—from her mother and father.

Not a week earlier, her mother had said it was a shame birthdays came whether you deserved them or not. She'd said she was dog-tired of Norah's disrespect, her ingratitude, her filthy language—as if *fucking* was just another word for *very*—fucking this and fucking that, fucking hot and fucking unfair and you have to be fucking kidding me.

And then there were a handful of nights when Norah didn't come home and turned off her phone so they all thought she was in the city in the apartment of some man she'd probably met on the internet and probably dead.

And then there were the horrible things she'd written about both her mother and father on Facebook.

And now they had to buy her presents?

I don't see that happening, Norah's mother had said.

So it was all a big surprise, and there was even a party. Her parents didn't approve of Norah's friends (and mostly didn't know who they were), so the party was just family. Norah's big sister brought the new baby, who yawned and hiccoughed and whose scalp was scaly with cradle cap. There was barbecued chicken and ears of corn cooked in milk, an ice cream cake with pralines and roses, and everyone, even Norah, was really careful and nice except for Norah's grandma, who had a fight in the kitchen with Norah's mother that stopped the minute Norah entered. Her grandmother gave Norah a kiss, wished her a happy birthday, and left before the food was served.

The party went late, and Norah's mother said they'd clean up in the morning. Everyone left or went to bed. Norah made a show of brushing her teeth, but she didn't undress, because Enoch and Kayla had said they'd come by, which they did, just before midnight. Enoch climbed through Norah's bedroom window, and then he tiptoed downstairs to the front door to let Kayla in, because she was already too trashed for the window. "Your birthday's not over yet!" Enoch said, and he'd brought Norah some special birthday shrooms called hawk's eyes. Half an hour later, the whole bedroom took a little skip sideways and broke open like an egg. Blue light poured over everything, and Norah's Care Bear, Milo, had a luminous blue aura, as if he were Yoda or something. Milo told Norah to tell Enoch she loved him, which made Enoch laugh.

They took more of the hawk's eyes, so Norah was still tripping the next morning when a man and a woman came into her bedroom, pulled her from her bed, and forced her onto her feet while her mother and father watched. The woman had a hooked nose and slightly protuberant eyeballs. Norah looked into her face just in time to see the fast retraction of a nictitating membrane. "Look at her eyes," she said, only the words came out of the woman's mouth instead of Norah's. "Look at her eyes," the woman said. "She's high as a kite."

Norah's mother collected clothes from the floor and the chair in the bedroom. "Put these on," she told Norah, but Norah couldn't find the sleeves, so the men left the room while her mother dressed her. Then the man and woman took her down the stairs and out the front door to a car so clean and black that clouds rolled across the hood. Norah's father put a suitcase in the trunk, and when he slammed it shut, the noise Norah heard was the last note in a Sunday school choir: the *men* part of *amen,* sung in many voices.

The music was calming. Her parents had been threatening to ship her off to boarding school for so long she'd stopped hearing it. Even now she thought that they were maybe all just trying to scare her, would drive her around for a bit and then bring her back, lesson learned, and this helped for a minute or two. Then she thought her mother wouldn't be crying in quite the way she was crying if it was all for show. Norah tried to grab her mother's arm, but missed. "Please," she started, "don't make me," but before she got the words out the man had leaned in to take them. "Don't make me hurt you," he said in a tiny whisper that echoed in her skull. He hand-cuffed Norah to the seatbelt because she was struggling. His mouth looked like something drawn onto his face with a charcoal pen.

"This is only because we love you," Norah's father said. "You were on a really dangerous path."

"This is the most difficult thing we've ever done," said Norah's mother. "Please be a good girl, and then you can come right home."

The man with the charcoal mouth and the woman with the nictitating eyelids drove Norah to an airport. They showed the woman at the ticket counter Norah's passport, and then they all got on a plane together, the woman in the window seat, the man, the aisle, and Norah in the middle. Sometime during the flight, Norah came down, and the man beside her had an ordinary face and the woman had ordinary eyes, but Norah was still on a plane with nothing beneath her but ocean.

While this was happening, Norah's mother drove to the mall. She had cried all morning, and now she was returning the iPod shuffle to the Apple store and the expensive clothes to Nordstrom. She had all her receipts, and everything still had the tags, plus she was sobbing intermittently, but uncontrollably, so there was no problem getting her money back.

• • •

Norah's new home was an old motel. She arrived after dark, the sky above pinned with stars and the road so quiet she could hear a bubbling chorus of frogs and crickets. The man held her arm and walked just fast enough to make Norah stumble. He let her fall onto one knee. The ground was asphalt covered with a grit that stuck in her skin and couldn't be brushed off. She was having trouble believing she was here. She was having trouble remembering the plane. It was a bad trip, a bad dream, as if she'd gone to bed in her bedroom as usual and awakened here. Her drugged-up visions of eyelids and mouths were forgotten; she was left with only a nagging suspicion she couldn't track back. But she didn't feel like a person being punished for bad behavior. She felt like an abductee.

An elderly woman in a flowered caftan met them at a chain-link gate. She unlocked it, and the man pushed Norah through without a word. "My suitcase," Norah said to the man, but he was already gone.

"Now I am your mother," the woman told Norah. She was very old, face like a crumpled leaf. "But not like your other mother. Two things different. One: I don't love you. Two: when I tell you what to do, you do it. You call me Mama Strong." Mama Strong stooped a little so she and Norah were eye to eye. Her pupils were tiny black beads. "You sleep now. We talk tomorrow."

They climbed an outside stairway, and Norah had just a glimpse of the moon-streaked ocean on the other side of the chainlink. Mama Strong took Norah to Room 217. Inside, ten girls were already in bed, the floor nearly covered with mattresses, only narrow channels of brown rug between. The light in the ceiling was on, but the girls' eyes were shut. A second old woman sat on a stool in the corner. She was sucking loudly on a red lollipop. "I don't have my toothbrush," Norah said.

"I didn't say brush your teeth," said Mama Strong. She gave Norah a yellow T-shirt, gray sweatpants, and plastic flip-flops, took her to the bathroom and waited for Norah to use the toilet, wash her face with tap water, and change. Then she took the clothes Norah had arrived in and went away.

The old woman pointed with her lollipop to an empty mattress, thin wool blanket folded at the foot. Norah lay down, covered herself with the blanket. The room was stuffy, warm, and smelled of the bodies in it. The mattress closest to Norah's belonged to a skinny black girl with a scabbed nose and a bad cough. Norah knew she was awake because of the coughing. "I'm

Norah," she whispered, but the old woman in the corner hissed and clapped her hands. It took Norah a long time to realize that no one was ever going to turn off the light.

Three times during the night she heard someone screaming. Other times she thought she heard the ocean, but she was never sure; it could have been a furnace or a fan.

In the morning, the skinny girl told Mama Strong that Norah had talked to her. The girl earned five points for this, which was enough to be given her hairbrush.

"I said no talking," Mama Strong told Norah.

"No, you didn't," said Norah.

"Who is telling the truth? You or me?" asked Mama Strong.

Norah, who hadn't eaten since the airplane or brushed her teeth in twenty-four hours, had a foul taste in her mouth like rotting eggs. Even so, she could smell the onions on Mama Strong's breath. "Me," said Norah.

She lost ten points for the talking and thirty for the talking back. This put her, on her first day, at minus forty. At plus ten she would have earned her toothbrush; at plus twenty, her hairbrush.

Mama Strong said that no talking was allowed anywhere—points deducted for talking—except at group sessions, where talking was required—points deducted for no talking. Breakfast was cold hard toast with canned peaches—points deducted for not eating—after which Norah had her first group session.

Mama Strong was her group leader. Norah's group was the girls from Room 217. They were, Norah was told, her new family. Her family name was Power. Other families in the hotel were named Dignity, Consideration, Serenity, and Respect. These were, Mama Strong said, not so good as family names. Power was the best.

There were boys in the west wings of the motel, but they wouldn't ever be in the yard at the same time as the girls. Everyone ate together, but there was no talking while eating, so they wouldn't be getting to know each other; anyway, they were all very bad boys. There was no reason to think about them at all, Mama Strong said.

She passed each of the Power girls a piece of paper and a pencil. She told them to write down five things about themselves that were true.

Norah thought about Enoch and Kayla, whether they knew where she had gone, what they might try to do about it. What she would do if it were them. She wrote: *I am a good friend. I am fun to be with.* Initially that was a single entry. Later when time ran out, she came back and made it two. She thought about her parents. *I am a picky eater*, she wrote on their behalf. She couldn't afford to be angry with them, not until she was home again. A mistake had been made. When her parents realized the kind of place this was, they would come and get her.

I am honest. I am stubborn, she wrote, because her mother had always said so. How many times had Norah heard how her mother spent eighteen hours in labor and finally had a C-section just because Fetal Norah wouldn't tuck her chin to clear the pubic bone. "If I'd known her then like I know her now," Norah's mother used to say, "I'd have gone straight to the C-section and spared myself the labor. 'This child is never going to tuck her chin,' I'd have said."

And then Norah scratched out the part about being stubborn, because she had never been so angry at her parents and she didn't want to give her mother the satisfaction. Instead she wrote, *Nobody knows who I really am.*

They were all to read their lists aloud. Norah was made to go first. Mama Strong sucked loudly through her teeth at number four. "Already this morning, Norah has lied to me two times," she told the group. "'I am honest' is the third lie today."

The girls were invited to comment. They did so immediately and with vigor. Norah seemed very stuck on herself, said a white girl with severe acne on her cheeks and chin. A red-haired girl with a freckled neck and freckled arms said that there was no evidence of Norah taking responsibility for anything. She agreed with the first girl. Norah was very stuck-up. The skinny girl with the cough said that no one honest ended up here. None of them were honest, but at least she was honest enough to admit it.

"I'm here by mistake," said Norah.

"Lie number four." Mama Strong reached over and took the paper, her eyes like stones. "*I* know who you really are," she said. "*I* know how you think. You think, how do I get out of here?

"*You* never will. The only way out is to be different. Change. Grow." She tore up Norah's list. "Only way is to be someone else completely. As long as some tiny place inside is still you, you will never leave."

The other girls took turns reading from their lists. "I am ungrateful," one of them had written. "I am a liar," read another. "I am still carrying around my bullshit," read the girl with the cough. "I am a bad person." "I am a bad daughter."

• • •

It took Norah three months to earn enough points to spend an afternoon outside. She stood blinking in the sun, watching a line of birds thread the sky above her. She couldn't see the ocean, but there was a breeze that brought the smell of salt.

Later she got to play kickball with the other Power girls in the old, drained motel pool. No talking, so they played with a silent ferocity, slamming each other into the pool walls until every girl was bleeding from the nose or the knee or somewhere.

After group there were classes. Norah would be given a lesson with a multiple-choice exercise. Some days it was math, some days history, geography, literature. At the end of an hour someone on staff would check her answers against a key. There was no instruction, and points were deducted for wrong answers. One day the lesson was the Frost poem "The Road Not Taken," which was not a hard lesson, but Norah got almost everything wrong, because the staff member was using the wrong key. Norah said so, and she lost points for her poor score, but also for the talking.

It took eleven months for Norah to earn enough points to write her parents. She'd known Mama Strong or someone else on staff would read the letter so she wrote it carefully. "Please let me come home. I promise to do whatever you ask and I think you can't know much about this place. I am sick a lot from the terrible food and have a rash on my legs from bug bites that keeps getting worse. I've lost weight. Please come and get me. I love you. Norah."

"So manipulative," Mama Strong had said. "So dishonest and manipulative." But she put the letter into an envelope and stamped it.

If the letter was dishonest, it was only by omission. The food here was not only terrible, it was unhealthy, often rotting, and there was never enough of it. Meat was served infrequently, so the students, hungry enough to eat anything, were always sick after. No more than three minutes every three hours could be spent on the toilet; there were always students whose legs were streaked with diarrhea. There was no medical care. The bug bites came from her mattress.

Sometimes someone would vanish. This happened to two girls in the Power family. One of them was the girl with the acne; her name was Kelsey. One of them was Jetta, a relatively new arrival. There was no explanation;

since no one was allowed to talk, there was no specula-
tion. Mama Strong had said if they earned a hundred
points they could leave. Norah tried to remember how
many points she'd seen Kelsey get; was it possible she'd
had a hundred? Not possible that Jetta did.

The night Jetta disappeared, there was a bloody
towel in the corner of the shower. Not just stained with
blood, soaked with it. It stayed in the corner for three
days until someone finally took it away.

A few weeks before her birthday, Norah lost all
her accumulated points, forty-five of them, for not going
deep in group session. By then Norah had no deep left.
She was all surface—skin rashes, eye infections, aching
teeth, constant hunger, stomach cramps. The people in
her life—the ones Mama Strong wanted to know everything about—had dimmed in her memory along with
everything else—school, childhood, all the fights with
her parents, all the Christmases, the winters, the sum-
mers, her fifteenth birthday. Her friends went first and
then her family.

The only things she could remember clearly were
those things she'd shared in group. Group session de-
manded ever more intimate, more humiliating, more
secret stories. Soon it seemed as if nothing had ever happened to Norah that wasn't shameful and painful. Worse,
her most secret shit was still found wanting, not suffi-
ciently revealing, dishonest.

Norah turned to vaguely remembered plots from
after-school specials until one day the story she was

telling was recognized by the freckled girl, Emilene was her name, who got twenty whole points for calling Norah on it.

There was a punishment called the TAP, the Think Again Position. Room 303 was the TAP room. It smelled of unwashed bodies and was crawling with ants. A student sent to the TAP was forced to lie face-down on the bare floor. Every three hours, a shift in position was allowed. A student who moved at any other time was put in restraint. Restraint meant that one staff member would set a knee on the student's spine. Others would pull the student's arms and legs back and up as far as they could go and then just a little bit farther. Many times a day, screaming could be heard in Room 303.

For lying in group session, Norah was sent to the TAP. She would be released, Mama Strong, said, when she was finally ready to admit that she was here as a result of her own decisions. Mama Strong was sick of Norah's games. Norah lasted two weeks.

"You have something to say?" Mama Strong was smoking a small hand-rolled cigarette that smelled of cinnamon. Smoke curled from her nostrils, and her fingers were stained with tobacco or coffee or dirt or blood.

"I belong here," Norah said.

"No mistake?"

"No."

"Just what you deserve?"

"Yes."

"Say it."

"Just what I deserve."

"Two weeks is nothing," Mama Strong said. "We had a girl three years ago, did eighteen."

Although it was the most painful, the TAP was not, to Norah's mind, the worst part. The worst part was the light that stayed on all night. Norah had not been in the dark for one single second since she arrived. The no dark was making Norah crazy. Her voice in group no longer sounded like her voice. It hurt to use it, hurt to hear it.

Her voice had betrayed her, telling Mama Strong everything until there was nothing left inside Norah that Mama Strong hadn't pawed through, like a shopper at a flea market. Mama Strong knew exactly who Norah was, because Norah had told her. What Norah needed was a new secret.

• • •

For her sixteenth birthday, she got two postcards. "We came all this way only to learn you're being disciplined and we can't see you. We don't want to be harsh on your birthday of all days, but honest to Pete, Norah, when are you going to have a change of attitude? Just imagine how disappointed we are." The handwriting was her father's, but the card had been signed by her mother and father both.

The other was written by her mother. "Your father said as long as we're here we might as well play tourist.

So now we're at a restaurant in the middle of the ocean. Well, maybe not the exact middle, but a long ways out! The restaurant is up on stilts on a sandbar and you can only get here by boat! We're eating a fish right off the line! All the food is so good, we envy you living here! Happy birthday, darling! Maybe next year we can celebrate your birthday here together. I will pray for that!" Both postcards had a picture of the ocean restaurant. It was called the Pelican Bar.

Her parents had spent five days only a few miles away. They'd swum in the ocean, drunk mai tais and mojitos under the stars, fed bits of bread to the gulls. They'd gone up the river to see the crocodiles and shopped for presents to take home. They were genuinely sorry about Norah; her mother had cried the whole first day and often after. But this sadness was heightened by guilt. There was no denying that they were happier at home without her. Norah had been a constant drain, a constant source of tension and despair. Norah left and peace arrived. The twins had never been difficult, but Norah's instructive disappearance had improved even their good behavior.

• • •

Norah is on her mattress in Room 217 under the overhead light, but she is also at a restaurant on stilts off the coast. She is drinking something made with rum. The sun is shining. The water is blue and rocking like a cradle. There is a breeze on her face.

Around the restaurant, nets and posts have been sunk into the sandbar. Pelicans sit on these or fly or sometimes drop into the water with their wings closed, heavy as stones. Norah wonders if she could swim all the way back in to shore. She's a good swimmer, or used to be, but this is merely hypothetical. She came by motorboat, trailing her hand in the water, and will leave the same way. Norah wipes her mouth with her hand, and her fingers taste of salt.

She buys a postcard. *Dear Norah*, she writes. *You could do the TAP better now. Maybe not for eighteen weeks, but probably more than two. Don't ever tell Mama Strong about the Pelican Bar, no matter what.*

For her sixteenth birthday what Norah got was the Pelican Bar.

• • •

Norah's seventeenth birthday passed without her noticing. She'd lost track of the date; there was just a morning when she suddenly thought that she must be seventeen by now. There'd been no card from her parents, which might have meant they hadn't sent one, but probably didn't. Their letters were frequent, if peculiar. They seemed to think there was water in the pool, fresh fruit at lunchtime. They seemed to think she had counselors and teachers and friends. They'd even made reference to college prep. Norah knew that someone on staff was writing and signing her name. It didn't matter. She could hardly remember her parents, didn't expect to ever see them again. Since "come and get me" hadn't worked, she had nothing further to say to them. Fine with her if someone else did.

One of the night women, one of the women who sat in the corner and watched while they slept, was younger than the others, with her hair in many braids. She took a sudden dislike to Norah. Norah had no idea why; there'd been no incident, no exchange, just an evening when the woman's eyes locked onto Norah's face and filled with poison. The next day she followed Norah through the halls and lobby, mewing at her like a cat. This went on until everyone on staff was mewing at Norah. Norah lost twenty points for it. Worse, she found it impossible to get to the Pelican Bar while everyone was mewing at her.

But even without Norah going there, Mama Strong could tell that she had a secret. Mama Strong paid less attention to the other girls and more to Norah, pushing and prodding in group, allowing the mewing even from the other girls, and sending Norah to the TAP again and again. Norah dipped back into minus points. Her hairbrush and her toothbrush were taken away. Her time in the shower was cut from five minutes to three. She had bruises on her thighs and a painful spot on her back where the knee went during restraint.

After several months without, she menstruated. The blood came in clots, gushes that soaked into her sweatpants. She was allowed to get up long enough to wash her clothes, but the blood didn't come completely out and the sweatpants weren't replaced. A man came and mopped the floor where Norah had to lie. It smelled strongly of piss when he was done.

More girls disappeared, until Norah noticed that she'd been there longer than almost anyone in the Power family. A new girl arrived and took the mattress and blanket Kimberly had occupied. The new girl's name was Chloe. The night she arrived, she spoke to Norah. "How long have you been here?" she asked. Her eyes were red and swollen, and she had a squashed kind of nose. She wasn't able to hold still; she jabbered about her meds which she hadn't taken and needed to; she rocked on the mattress from side to side.

"The new girl talked to me last night," Norah told Mama Strong in the morning. Chloe was a born victim, gave off the victim vibe. She was so weak, it was like a superpower. The kids at her school had bullied her, she said in group session, like this would be news to anyone.

"Maybe you ask for it," Emilene suggested.

"Why don't you take responsibility?" Norah said. "Instead of blaming everyone else."

"You will learn to hold still," Mama Strong told her and had the girls put her in restraint themselves. Norah's was the knee in her back.

Then Mama Strong told them all to make a list of five reasons they'd been sent here. "I am a bad daughter," Norah wrote. "I am still carrying around my bullshit. I am ungrateful." And then her brain snapped shut like a clamshell so she couldn't continue.

"There is something else you want to say." Mama Strong stood in front of her, holding the incriminating paper, two reasons short of the assignment, in her hand.

She was asking for Norah's secret. She was asking about the Pelican Bar. "No," said Norah. "It's just that I can't think."

"Tell me." The black beads of Mama Strong's eyes became pinpricks. "Tell me. Tell me." She stepped around Norah's shoulder so that Norah could smell onion and feel a cold breath on her neck, but couldn't see her face.

"I don't belong here," Norah said. She was trying to keep the Pelican Bar. To do that, she had to give Mama Strong something else. There was probably a smarter plan, but Norah couldn't think of anything. "Nobody belongs here," she said. "This isn't a place where humans belong."

"You are human, but not me?" Mama Strong said. Mama Strong had never touched Norah. But her voice coiled like a spring; she made Norah flinch. Norah felt her own piss on her thighs.

"Maybe so," Mama Strong said. "Maybe I'll send you somewhere else then. Say you want that. Ask me for it. Say it and I'll do it."

Norah held her breath. In that instant, her brain produced the two missing reasons. "I am a liar," she said. She heard her own desperation. "I am a bad person."

There was a silence, and then Norah heard Chloe saying she wanted to go home. Chloe clapped her hands over her mouth. Her talking continued, only now no one could make out the words. Her head nodded like a bobblehead dog on a dashboard.

Mama Strong turned to Chloe. Norah got sent to the TAP, but not to Mama Strong's someplace else.

• • •

After that, Mama Strong never again seemed as interested in Norah. Chloe hadn't learned yet to hold still, but Mama Strong was up to the challenge. When Norah was seventeen, the gift she got was Chloe.

One day, Mama Strong stopped Norah on her way to breakfast. "Follow me," she said, and led Norah to the chain-link fence. She unlocked the gate and swung it open. "You can go now." She counted out fifty dollars. "You can take this and go. Or you can stay until your mother and father come for you. Maybe tomorrow. Maybe next week. You go now, you get only as far as you get with fifty dollars."

Norah began to shake. This, she thought, was the worst thing done to her yet. She took a step toward the gate, took another. She didn't look at Mama Strong. She saw that the open gate was a trick, which made her shaking stop. She was not fooled. Norah would never be allowed to walk out. She took a third step and a fourth. "You don't belong here," Mama Strong said with contempt, as if there'd been a test and Norah had flunked it. Norah didn't know if this was because she'd been too compliant or not compliant enough.

And then Norah was outside and Mama Strong was closing and locking the gate behind her.

Norah walked in the sunlight down a paved road dotted with potholes and the smashed skins of frogs. The road curved between weeds taller than Norah's head, bushes with bright orange flowers. Occasionally a car went by, driven very fast.

Norah kept going. She passed stucco homes, some small stores. She saw cigarettes and muumuus for sale, large avocados, bunches of small bananas, liquor bottles filled with dish soap, posters for British ale. She thought about buying something to eat, but it seemed too hard, would require her to talk. She was afraid to stop walking. It was very hot on the road in the sun. A pack of small dogs followed her briefly and then ran back to wherever they'd come from.

She reached the ocean and walked into the water. The salt stung the rashes on her legs, the sores on her arms, and then it stopped stinging. The sand was brown, the water blue and warm. She'd forgotten about the fifty dollars though she was still holding them in her hand, now soaked and salty.

There were tourists everywhere on the beach, swimming, lying in the sun with daiquiris and ice cream sandwiches and salted oranges. She wanted to tell them that, not four miles away, children were being starved and terrified. She couldn't remember enough about people to know if they'd care. Probably no one would believe her. Probably they already knew.

She waded in to shore and walked farther. It was so hot, her clothes dried quickly. She came to a river and an open-air market. A young man with a scar on his cheek approached her. She recognized him. On two occasions, he'd put her in restraint. Her heart began to knock against her lungs. The air around her went black.

"Happy birthday," he said.

He came swimming back into focus, wearing a bright plaid shirt, smiling so his lip rose like a curtain over his teeth. He stepped toward her; she stepped away. "Your birthday, yes?" he said. "Eighteen?" He bought her some bananas, but she didn't take them.

A woman behind her was selling beaded bracelets, peanuts, and puppies. She waved Norah over. "True," she said to Norah. "At eighteen, they have to let you go. The law says." She tied a bracelet onto Norah's wrist. How skinny Norah's arm looked in it. "A present for your birthday," the woman said. "How long were you there?"

Instead of answering, Norah asked for directions to the Pelican Bar. She bought a T-shirt, a skirt, and a cola. She drank the cola, dressed in the new clothes, and threw away the old. She bought a ticket on a boat—ten dollars it cost her to go, ten more to come back. There were tourists, but no one sat anywhere near her.

The boat dropped her, along with the others, twenty feet or so out on the sandbar, so that she walked the last bit through waist-high water. She was encircled by the straight, clean line of the horizon, the whole world spinning around her, flat as a plate. The water was a brilliant, sun-dazzled blue in every direction. She twirled slowly, her hands floating, her mind flying until it was her turn on the makeshift ladder of planks and branches and her grip on the wood suddenly anchored her. She climbed into the restaurant in her dripping dress.

She bought a postcard for Chloe. "On your eighteenth birthday, come here," she wrote, "and eat a fish right off the line. I'm sorry about everything. I'm a bad person."

She ordered a fish for herself, but couldn't finish it. She sat for hours, feeling the floor of the bar rocking beneath her, climbing down the ladder into the water and up again to dry in the warm air. She never wanted to leave this place that was the best place in the world, even more beautiful than she'd imagined. She fell asleep on the restaurant bench and didn't wake up until the last boat was going to shore and someone shook her arm to make sure she was on it.

When Norah returned to shore, she saw Mama Strong seated in an outdoor bar at the edge of the market on the end of the dock. The sun was setting and dark coming on. Mama Strong was drinking something that could have been water or could have been whiskey. The glass was colored blue, so there was no way to be sure. She saw Norah getting off the boat. There was no way back that didn't take Norah toward her.

"You have so much money, you're a tourist?" Mama Strong asked. "Next time you want to eat, the money is gone. What then?"

Two men were playing the drums behind her. One of them began to sing. Norah recognized the tune—something old that her mother had liked—but not the words.

"Do you think I'm afraid to go hungry?" Norah said.

"So. We made you tougher. Better than you were. But not tough enough. Not what we're looking for. You go be whatever you want now. Have whatever you want. We don't care."

What did Norah want to be? Clean. Not hungry. Not hurting. What did she want to have? She wanted to sleep in the dark. Already there was one bright star in the sky over the ocean.

What else? She couldn't think of a thing. Mama Strong had said Norah would have to change, but Norah felt that she'd vanished instead. She didn't know who she was anymore. She didn't know anything at all. She fingered the beaded bracelet on her wrist. "When I run out of money," she said, "I'll ask someone to help me. And someone will. Maybe not the first person I ask. But someone." Maybe it was true.

"Very pretty." Mama Strong looked into her blue glass, swirled whatever was left in it, tipped it down her throat. "You're wrong about humans, you know," she said. Her tone was conversational. "Humans do everything we did. Humans do more."

Two men came up behind Norah. She whirled, sure that they were here for her, sure that she'd be taken, maybe back, maybe to Mama Strong's more horrible someplace else. But the men walked right past her, toward the drummers. They walked right past her and as they walked, they began to sing. Maybe they were human and maybe not.

"Very pretty world," said Mama Strong.

"MORE EXUBERANT THAN IS STRICTLY TASTEFUL"

KAREN JOY FOWLER INTERVIEWED BY TERRY BISSON

Do they really put chopped nuts in sushi in Santa Cruz?

It's one of the town's many charms.

There is a rumor that L. Ron Hubbard played a role in your development as a writer. Explain.

My story "Recalling Cinderella" was published in *Writers of the Future*, an anthology funded by Scientology. This was my first publication, though not my first sale; the Scientologists proved more efficient than Ed Ferman, editor of *Fantasy & Science Fiction*. The anthology was made up of winners in a quarterly contest. I did not even place. But Algis Budrys, who edited the volume, liked my story enough to include it. So I would say that Algis

Budrys had an impact on my career but that L. Ron Hubbard found me wanting.

This all happened in that particular period in which L. Ron Hubbard was maybe dead or maybe not dead. There was an extravagant launch party in LA where I met many science fiction writers of whom I was in breathless admiration. The party and my thirty-fifth birthday were on the same day, so I hardly minded turning thirty-five. Many days of sorrow would have been avoided if the Scientologists had also thrown me a big party when I turned forty.

Several of your works I would describe as historicals. Certainly The Sweetheart Season, Sarah Canary, *and* Sister Noon. *Does the research come before or after the idea?*

The research begins long before the writing, years before, but continues throughout. Initially, I just free-read through the period, looking for things I can use, elements that will shape and adorn the story. If I find an interesting setting, well described, I will steer my story into that space for a scene or two. I make decisions about the story I'll tell based on the things I've been able to find.

Later I have specific needs. I might want to know what the residents of the Steilacoom insane asylum ate or what chewing gum looked like in 1871 or how radioactive the atomic ring you could buy from the back of the magazines actually was.

There was a time when approaching the desk of the research librarians at UC Davis was like Norm entering Cheers. "Where everybody knows your name . . ."

How often do you go to the movies?

About once a week. That's in the winter; we go less in the summer. One of the things that drew me initially to my husband was that we both believed seeing a bad movie was better than seeing no movie at all. Now we're old and cranky and have changed our minds about that—but we both changed our minds together, which is how a marriage must work when the initial contract is so substantially altered.

And suddenly, these days, television is better than the movies—more interesting, more original, more compelling. What science fiction writer saw *that* one coming?

The title of your newest novel is We Are All Completely Beside Ourselves. *Why* completely? *Why, for that matter,* all? *The title seems to be saying more than simply nonplussed.*

All is, of course, necessary, because, though I am the one raising the issue here, it is most certainly not just me. Not just my narrator and me. Though she has lived an extreme version of being beside herself, still, it affects us all.

Completely addresses the magnitude of the situation. Everywhere we go, there we are. Surrounded. Us to the right of us, us to the left. Nowhere we are not once we've gotten there.

The line between us and not-us is a blurry one: that's what the title is trying to say. This is partly because we are incapable of seeing anything that isn't transformed into us by the mere act of seeing it. And partly because we are all part of Darwin's world.

Does that clear things up? Surely it must. Nonplussed is the least important part.

Many of your works have what I would call an exemplary aspect. Is this to add an old-fashioned patina, or is it a natural ingredient of SF? Or do you just think people need fixing?

People need so much fixing. It's exhausting, honestly. And unappreciated.

"Hey! You there! Shape up!"

See what I mean? I hardly have time to be interviewed, there is so much fixing to be done.

You were one of the founders of the famously feminist James Tiptree Award. Why is it named after a guy?

Technically the Tiptree is not a feminist award. In theory it could go to a work of severe antifeminism as long as the antifeminism was interesting, innovative, and original, and not the same old tired claptrap. But little is new in the world of antifeminism. I can't help but feel they are phoning it in.

So feminist works usually end up winning the award.

It's named after SF writer Alice Sheldon, who made up a man, James Tiptree Jr., to write her science fiction stories for her.

"The Pelican Bar" is pretty scary. Where'd that idea come from? Guantánamo?

Definitely Guantánamo. Also Abu Ghraib. But even more directly, from the chain of overseas schools run by the World Wide Association of Specialty Programs and Schools (WWASPS), particularly the notorious Tranquility Bay in Jamaica and High Impact in Mexico. I read online a statement that we shouldn't be surprised that Americans are OK with torturing foreign prisoners, because apparently we are OK with the torturing of American children, as long as it happens overseas. That statement was the seed of my story.

What kind of car do you drive? I already know but am required to ask.

Like everyone else in Santa Cruz, I drive a silver Prius. I take it downtown to pick up my sushi with nuts.

In What I Didn't See, *your short story collection from Small Beer Press, a narrator declares, "The older I get, the more I want a happy ending." Is that a promise or a threat?*

It's a plea.

You have success in both short and long form, stories and novels. Do you go at them differently?

I love writing short stories best. They are so manageable. By the time I finish one, I know how it works, how it's been put together. I feel like a clockmaker.

Novels are just a mess. I never have a sense of the whole; I never am sure what I've achieved or what I've failed to achieve. But I do like spending more time with my characters, which a novel affords. I miss my characters when I finish a novel. I don't miss the ones from my short stories.

Ever been attacked by drones?

No, but they stalk me. I see them out of the corners of my eyes.

Maxwell Lane, your imaginary imaginary [sic] *detective in* Wit's End, *recommends asking at least one question that won't be answered. What would that be for you?*

What happened to Beverly in my story "What I Didn't See"?

What's the deal with all the apes? I was a little surprised when one didn't show up in The Jane Austen Book Club. *I didn't say disappointed.*

You do understand that you and I are apes? Great apes, which takes the sting out.

So both of us have apes galore, only your stories have more bears. Even just articulating that makes me suddenly feel all competitive. Note to self: write more stories with bears. Don't cede the bears to Bisson.

Here's my Jeopardy question: I provide the answer, you provide the question. A: Small boys with big ideas.

Q: What's even scarier than drones?

If you weren't a writer what would you be, as in do?

I would go on anthropological digs and find amazing pottery shards. I would study cave paintings and also elephants in the wild. I would restore old books, damaged by weather and fire. I would sail around the world. I would be such a valuable member of society that you would hardly recognize me.

Is it true that Sarah Canary *was originally titled* Sister from Another Planet?

Something should be titled *Sister from Another Planet*. It would be nice if I didn't have to write it myself, but I am here, waiting and eager to read it. Doesn't this seem like a job for Eleanor Arnason? I think she might be just the woman for it. I would read *Sister from Another Planet* by Eleanor Arnason in a heartbeat.

What do you think California will look like in 150 years?

More salt water, less fresh. Water wars all up and down the state. It's Chinatown, Jake.

One of your favorite plot devices is "nice girl gets falling-down drunk." Did you steal that or make it up?

It's a standard romcom trope. See *The Philadelphia Story*, *The Sure Thing*, *The Cutting Edge*, countless others. The woman cannot admit her true feelings until she gets drunk. Because these are movies and not life, the man refuses to take advantage of the situation. Sometimes the woman is angry about this refusal and true love is delayed yet again as a result.

So I've just taken this same trope and am using it in non-romcoms. No one is in love. No one is learning anything about their true feelings through the magic of alcohol. In my books, people are simply getting drunk. I am subverting the genre. It's possible I'm drinking heavily as I do so.

Have you ever been arrested? Were you eventually released?

By the time I joined the revolution, the police had stopped arresting us. It was seen as pointless since the courts just released us again back into the wild first chance they got. So the police were beating us up instead and skipping the arresting part. I've never been arrested, but I've been beaten up.

I've also been rescued by the police in other contexts. It's all been very confusing.

But I *am* clear now that my constitutional rights are not meant to be actually, you know, exercised.

What are you reading this week?

Snapper by Brian Kimberling. So recommended!

Your thoughts on each in one sentence please: John Crowley, Agnes Smedley, David Sedaris, Molly Gloss, Evelyn Waugh.

I can name that tune in one word. Brilliant, inspiring, hilarious, impeccable, eternal. You can pretty much rotate the adjectives, give them a spin, as they apply equally to all of the above.

Do you have a regular drill as a writer? Ever work in longhand?

I can't work in longhand. I get too involved with penmanship. I become a monk with an illuminated manuscript.

My regular drill is to intend to write and then spend the day sitting at my computer doing my e-mail and browsing my favorite sites instead. Watching some TED talks. I love TED talks. They are the only place where I find hope for the future. But then I spoil the mood by scoping out the political scene. All the while filled with a faint but ineffective self-loathing because I'm not writing.

Why do drivers wait so long to start moving when the light changes?

They're on the phone.

You have a solid reputation in genre (SF) and in mainstream as well. Does that ever make for a conflict?

Do I? A *solid* reputation? Are you sure? It seems to me that the question of whether I write genre fiction at all has dogged me my whole career. I was very pleased when *Locus* publisher Charles Brown told me years ago that of course I was a science fiction writer. It didn't matter *what* I wrote, he said, because I *thought* like a science fiction writer.

I do love genre fiction. I also love mainstream literary fiction. As a reader sometimes I want one and sometimes I want the other. There is no reason not to read both.

As a writer, sometimes I want to write one and sometimes the other, but this has been trickier. When I began publishing, NY believed that either people read science fiction and nothing else, or they never read science fiction. Scrupulous attention was paid to my positioning and though it never seemed like a problem to me, I was aware that it seemed like a problem to others.

It probably was a problem. It has been my great good fortune not to have to spend much time thinking about it.

The social world of science fiction has been extremely welcoming to me. I do truly want someday to repay that kindness by writing a book in the genre for those steadfast friends and readers. But guess what? Genre fiction is very hard to write well.

What do you like doing best, first draft or revisions?

I hate the first, fumbling, dispiriting draft. Team Revision all the way.

Tarantino, as in the name of the film director, originally meant citizen of Tarentum, the ancient Greek city in Southern Italy. Did you know that?

I know it now.

You teach in lots of writing workshops, and with some apparent success. What's your emphasis there? What do writers leave with that they came without?

How would you measure success as a workshop teacher? I try first to do no harm. I make my best possible effort to see the story the writer is trying to tell and help them achieve that. I try very hard not to confuse their story with the story I would be telling, given that same material. Sometimes I fail at that, but not for lack of effort.

I believe that the learning in workshops happens to the critiquer not the critiqued. So I do demand that my students put careful attention into their responses as readers. As writers I caution them not to make changes based on the critiques they get unless they see clearly how that will improve the story they want to tell.

And I also provide such craft tips as have worked for me over the years. It's been a bit strange, or was at first, to look closely my own process, because most of it was happening unconsciously. In order to teach, I've had to observe myself at work. It's not always a pretty sight.

Who do you think would win in a fight, Dr. Johnson or Jane Austen? A footrace?

Austen would refuse to compete. Johnson would win, but he would look such a fool for having done so.

Ever do any hack work? What sort?

Nothing literary, but I once spent a summer sorting tomatoes for Hunt and Wesson. I was not good at this. The potential for advancement to catsup labels was always there and always out of reach. I turned out to be too picky about the tomatoes I wanted in my tomato sauce.

I was also pregnant at the time and suffering from morning sickness. I couldn't eat tomatoes for years.

Even now, the smell of mountains of off-peak tomatoes streaming past on conveyor belts haunts my dreams.

Do you read on the Kindle?

I read on the iPad, but only when I travel. I persist in liking books on paper best. I've learned that the sense of how close to the end of a book I am, which no electronic version can recreate for me in quite that same physical way, is an important component of my reading experience.

Carter Scholz claims he had a role in the development of The Jane Austen Book Club. *Is this true, or just another of his tall tales?*

There would be no *Jane Austen Book Club* without Carter Scholz. That's the plain and simple truth of the matter. I was at a bookstore with Carter when I misread the sign that gave me the title.

You spent your early youth in Indiana. Do you like James Whitcomb Riley?

I was kept away from the great Hoosier poet as a child. My parents surely had their reasons and I never developed a taste for him and his homespun dialect. The Hoosier poet my parents did approve of was Samuel Yellen, and they read to me often from his book *In the House and*

Out. Especially at bedtime. "It's time to take your place in Cassiopeia's chair" (or something very like that). This was a poem about the constellations, very beautiful and starry. Put me right to sleep.

What authors do you think have had the most influence on your work?

T.H. White, by a mile. Author of *The Once and Future King*. T.H. White is why I have never believed that I had to follow the rules or consider anything resembling a "contract with the reader." T.H. White is why I never believed that I had to pick a single genre or a single tone or choose between comedy and tragedy, between historical and contemporary, between realistic and fantastical. No reason not to do them all and all the time, either piece by piece or within the same work or within the same paragraph. T.H. White taught me that writing can be more exuberant than is strictly tasteful, and I like exuberance best, though I'm not sure I often achieve it.

Do you read poetry for fun?

I do. For fun and for fuel. The innovative use of language is inspiring to me. It makes me want to write, which is a helpful first step in writing.

I understand that you are the only science fiction writer in the Baseball Hall of Fame. Is that fair?

Nothing in baseball is fair or foul but thinking makes it so.

Actually, I'm not *in* the Baseball Hall of Fame. I merely have my own key to the door. They gave it to me because my novel *The Sweetheart Season* was about a women's baseball team. At least in part.

What did you think of the film of The Jane Austen Book Club? *You are allowed to dissemble on this one.*

There are parts of the movie I think work really, really well. Some of those parts come straight from my book, but many do not.

There are also parts I don't care for. I don't believe reading Austen aloud can save a marriage. I don't believe a high school teacher should sit in the car necking with a student no matter how poorly she was mothered. My characters would never behave so badly.

And it is tiring to have people approach, as they quite often do, to tell me what they loved about my book, only to realize they are talking about the movie. If I persuade the people reading this of one thing, let it be that. The writer is going to know if you pretend to have read the book when you've only seen the movie. Don't even try.

But all in all, I like the movie. It's not my book, but it's smart and entertaining and there is a scene (not in my book) in which a nice woman gets falling-down drunk, which is, as already established, the mark of great storytelling.

What will your memorial bench say?

Hey! You, there! Shape up!

THE FURTHER ADVENTURES OF THE INVISIBLE MAN

—FOR RYAN

MY MOTHER LIKES TO refer to 1989 as the year I played baseball, as if she had nothing to do with it, as if nothing *she* did that year was worth noting. She has her unamended way with too many of the facts of our lives, especially those occurring before I was born, about which there is little I can do. But this one is truly unfair. My baseball career was short, unpleasant, and largely her fault.

For purposes of calibration where my mother's stories are concerned, you should know that she used to say my father had been abducted by aliens. My mother and he made a pact after *Close Encounters of the Third Kind* that if one of them got the chance they should just go and the other would understand, so she figured right away that this is what had happened. He hadn't known

I was coming yet or all bets would have been off, my mother said.

This was before *X-Files* gave alien abduction a bad name; even so my mother said we didn't need to go telling everyone. There'd be plenty of time for that when he returned, which he would be doing, of course. If he could. It might be tricky. If the aliens had faster-than-light spaceships, then he wouldn't be aging at the same rate as we; he might even be growing younger; no one knew for sure how these things worked. He might come back as a boy like me. Or it was entirely possible that he would have to transmutate his physical body into a beam of pure light in order to get back to us, which, honestly, wasn't going to do us a whole lot of good and he probably should just stay put. In any case, he wouldn't want us pining away, waiting for him—he would want us to get on with our lives. So that's what we were doing and none of this is about my father.

My mother worked as a secretary over at the college in the department of anthropology. Sometimes she referred to this job as her fieldwork. I could write a book, she would tell Tamara and me over dinner, I could write a book about that department that would call the whole theory of evolution into question. Tamara lived with us to help pay the rent. She looked like Theda Bara, though of course I didn't know that back then. She wore peasant blouses and ankle bracelets and rings in her ears. She slept in the big bedroom and worked behind the counter at Cafe Roma and sometimes sang on open mike night.

She never did her dishes, but that was okay, my mom said. Tamara got enough of that at work and we couldn't afford not to be understanding. The dishes could be *my* job.

My other job was to go to school, which wasn't so easy in the sixth grade when this particular installment takes place. A lot of what made it hard was named Jeremy Campbell. You have to picture me, sitting in my first row desk, all hopeful attention. I just recently gave up my Inspector Gadget lunchbox for a nonpartisan brown bag. I'm trying to fit in. But that kid with the blond hair who could already be shaving, that's Jeremy Campbell. He's at the front of the room, so close I could touch him, giving his book report.

"But it's too late," Jeremy says, looking at me to be sure I know he's looking at me. "Every single person in that house is dead." He turns to Mrs. Gruber. "That's the end."

"I guess it would have to be," Mrs. Gruber says. "Are you sure this is a book you read? This isn't just some story you heard at summer camp?"

"*The Meathook Murders.*"

"Written by?"

Jeremy hesitates a moment. "King."

"Stephen King?"

"Stanley King."

"It's not on the recommended list."

Jeremy shakes his head sadly. "I can't explain that. It's the best book I ever read."

"All right," says Mrs. Gruber. "Take your seat, Jeremy."

On his way past my desk Jeremy deliberately knocks my books onto the floor. "Are you trying to trip me, Nathan?" he asks.

"Take your seat, Jeremy," Mrs. Gruber says.

"I'll talk to you later," Jeremy assures me.

• • •

After school, having no friends to speak of, I sometimes biked to my mom's office. The bike path between my school and hers took me past the Little League fields, the Mormon temple, some locally famous hybrid trees—a very messy half walnut–half elm created by Luther Burbank himself just to see if he could—and the university day care, where I once spent all day every day finger painting and was a much happier camper.

I came to a stop sign at the same time as a woman in a minivan. (Maybe this was the same day as Jeremy's book report, maybe not. I include it so you'll know the sort of town we live in.) Even though I came to a complete stop, even though I didn't know her from Adam, she rolled down her window to talk to me. "You should be wearing a helmet," she said. *That* kind of town. Someone had graffitied the words BASEBALL SPAWNS HATE onto the Little League snack bar. This is a story about baseball, remember?

My mom's desk was in the same room as the faculty mailboxes. A busy place, but she liked that, she always liked to talk to people. On my way into the office I passed one of the other secretaries and two profs. By the time I got to my mom I'd been asked three times how school was and three times I'd said it was fine. There was a picture of me on her desk, taken when I was three and wearing a Batman shirt with the batwings stretched over my fat little three-year-old stomach, and also my most recent school picture, no matter how bad.

"Hey, cookie." My mom was always happy to see me; it's still one of the things I like best about her. "How was school?" I think she was pretty, but most kids think that about their moms; maybe she wasn't. Her hair was blond back then and cut extremely short, her eyes a light, light blue. She had a little snow globe on her desk only instead of a snow scene there was a miniature copy of the sphinx inside, and instead of snow there was gold glitter. I picked it up and shook it.

"Have you ever heard of a book called *The Meathook Murders*?" I asked. I was just making conversation. Mom's not much of a reader.

Sure enough, she hadn't. But it reminded her of a movie she'd seen and she started to tell me the plot, which took some time, being complicated and featuring nuns with hooks for hands. My mom went to Catholic school.

She kept forgetting bits of it and the whole time she was talking to me she was also typing a letter, up until the climax, which required both hands. My mom showed me how the sleeve of the habit fell so that you saw the hook, but only for a second, and then the nun said, "Are you here to confess?" just to get into the confessional where no one could see. And then it turned out not to be the nun with the hook, after all. It turned out to be the policeman, dressed in the wimple with a fake hook. He ended up stabbed with his own fake hook, which was, my mom assured me, a very satisfying conclusion.

Somewhere in the middle of her recitation Professor Knight came in to pick up his mail. Back in the fifth grade, during the Christmas concert, when we all had reindeer horns on our heads and jingle bells in our hands and our parents were there to see us, Bjorn Benson told me that Professor Knight was my father. "Everyone knows," Bjorn said. But Professor Knight had a daughter named Kate who was just a year older than me, and I'm betting she didn't know, nor his wife neither. Kate and I were at the same school then, where I could keep an eye on her. But by now she was at the junior high and I only saw her downtown sometimes. She was a skinny girl with cow eyes who sucked on her hair. "Stop staring at me" is about the only thing she ever said to me. She didn't *look* like my sister.

I kept meaning to ask my mom, but I kept chickening out. I wasn't ever really supposed to believe in the alien abduction story; it was just there to be something funny to say, but mainly to stop me asking anything outright. Which I certainly couldn't do then, not when she was working so hard to keep me distracted and entertained. Besides, Professor Knight didn't even glance our way; if he was my father I think he would've wanted to know how school was. But then I was suspicious all over again, because the moment he left, my mom started talking about my dad. The wonders he was seeing! The friends he was making! "On the planet Zandoor," she told me, "they only wish they had hooks for hands. Instead, they have herrings. Your dad could get stuck there a long time just dialing their phones for them."

She ran out of steam, all at once, her mouth sagging so she looked sad and tired. My response to this was complicated. I felt sorry for her, but it made me angry, too. I was just a kid, it didn't seem fair to make me see this. So I gave her the note Mrs. Gruber had said to take right home to her a couple of weeks ago. I was just being mean. I'd already read it. It said Mrs. Gruber wondered if I didn't need a male role model.

And then I was relieved that Mom didn't seem to mind. She crumpled the note and hooked it over her head into the wastebasket. "I've got a job to do, cupcake," she said, so I went home and played *The Legend of Zelda* until dinnertime.

•••

But she was more upset than she let on. Later that night Victor Wong dropped by, and I heard them talking. Victor worked in the computer department at Pacific Gas and Electric and was my mom's best friend. He was a thin-faced, delicate guy. I liked him a lot, maybe partly because he was the one man I knew for sure wasn't my dad—wrong race—and wasn't ever going to be my dad. He'd been coming around for a long time without it getting romantic. I always thought he liked Tamara though he never said so, even to my mom. If you believe her.

"Hey, don't look at me," Victor said when she brought up Mrs. Gruber's note. "I'm a heterosexual man and everyone who meets me assumes I'm gay. I'm a hopeless failure at both lifestyles."

"There's not a damn thing wrong with Nathan," my mom said, which was nice of her, especially since she didn't know I was listening. "He's a great kid. He's never given me a speck of trouble. Where does she get off?"

"Maybe the note wasn't aimed at Nathan. Maybe the note was aimed at you."

"I don't know what you're talking about."

"I think you do," Victor said. But I certainly didn't, although I spent a fair amount of time puzzling over it. I could make a better guess now. Apparently my mother used to flirt outrageously during PTA meetings in a way some people felt distracted from the business at hand. Or so Bjorn Benson says. He's still a font of information, but he's a CPA now. I doubt he'd lie.

"How you doing, Nathan?" Victor asked me later on his way to the bathroom. I was still playing *The Legend of Zelda*.

"I just need a magic sword," I told him.

"Who doesn't?" he said.

• • •

This brings us up to Saturday afternoon. The car wouldn't start; it put my mom in a very bad mood. She was always sure our mechanic was ripping her off. She had a date that evening, a fix-up from a friend, some guy named Michael she'd never even seen. So I left her getting ready and biked over to Bertilucci's Lumber and Drugs. My plan was to price a new game called *The Adventure of Link*. Even though I was such a great kid, and had never given her a speck of trouble, my mother had steadily refused to buy this game for me. I already spent too much time playing *The Legend of Zelda*, she said, as if getting me *The Adventure of Link* wouldn't solve that problem in a hot second. Anyway we couldn't afford it, especially not now that the car had to be repaired again.

Somewhere in the distance, a farmer was burning his fields. The sky to the south was painted with smoke and the whole town smelled sweetly of it. On my way to the store I passed the Yamaguchis'. Ms. Yamaguchi took self-defense with my mother and was very careful about gender-engendering toys. Her four-year-old son, Davey, was on the porch with his doll. As I biked by, he held the doll up, sighted along it. "Ack-ack-ack-ack," he said, picking me off cleanly.

I spent maybe fifteen minutes mooning over the video games. I wanted *The Adventure of Link* so bad I didn't even notice that Jeremy Campbell had come into the store, although if I'd looked into the shoplifting mirrors I could've seen him before he snuck up behind me. He put a hand on my shoulder and spun me around. He was with Diego Ruiz, a kid who'd never been anything but nice to me till this. "Come with me," Jeremy said.

We went to the front of the store where Mr. Bertilucci had temporarily abandoned the counter and Jeremy went around it and pulled the new copy of *Playboy* out from underneath. "Have you ever seen this before?" he asked me. He'd already flipped open the centerfold and he put it right on my face; I was actually breathing into her breasts, which was maybe all that kept me from hyperventilating.

"My mom says I have to get right home," I told him.

"Do pictures of naked women always make you think of your mom?" he asked. "Does your mom have tits like these?"

"I've seen his mom," Diego said. "No tits at all."

"Sad." Jeremy put an arm around me. "I'll tell you what," he said.

"Take this magazine out of the store for me"—he tucked it inside my jacket while he talked—"and I'll owe you one."

I would have offered to buy it, but I didn't have money and Mr. Bertilucci wouldn't have sold it to me if I did. I really didn't see how I had a choice in the matter so I zipped my jacket up, but then it occurred to me that if I was going to shoplift anyway I should get something I wanted, so I went back for *The Adventure of Link*.

Soon I was at the police department, talking with a cop named Officer Harper. I got my one phone call and caught my mom just as she and Michael were about to leave the house. Since my mom had no car she was forced to ask Michael to drive her to the police station. Since they were planning on a classy restaurant she arrived in her blue dress with dangly earrings in the shape of golden leaves, shoes with tiny straps, and heels that clicked when she walked, tea rose perfume on her neck. Michael had long hair and a Star Trek tie.

We all sat and watched a videotape of me sticking the game under my jacket. Apparently most theft occurred at the video games; it was the only part of the store televised. There was no footage at all of Jeremy, at least none that we saw. I was more scared of Jeremy than Officer Harper, so I kept my mouth shut. Officer Harper told my mom and Michael to call him Dusty.

"He's never done anything like this before, Dusty," my mom said. "He's a great kid."

Dusty had a stern look for me, a concerned one for my mother. "You and your husband," he began.

"I'm not her husband," Michael said.

"Where's his father?"

Apparently we weren't telling the police about the alien abduction. "He's not part of the picture," was all my mother would say about that. "Is there any other man taking an interest in him?" Dusty asked. He was looking at Michael.

"Christ." Michael blocked the look with his hands, waved them about. "This is our first date. This is me, meeting the kid for the first time. How do you do, Nathan."

"Don't kids with fathers ever shoplift?" my mother asked. She was looking so nice, but her voice had a tight-wound sound to it.

"I'm only asking because of the *Playboy*." Dusty had confiscated the magazine and inventoried it with the other officers. Now he put it, folded up discreetly, on the metal desk between us.

This was the first my mother had heard about the *Playboy*. I could see her taking it in and, unhappy as she already was, I could see it made an impact. "I do have a suggestion," Dusty said.

It was a terrible suggestion. Dusty coached a Little League team called the Tigers. He thought Mr. Bertilucci might not press charges if Dusty could tell him he'd be keeping a personal eye on me. "I don't like baseball," I said. I was very clear about this. I would rather have gone to jail.

"A whole team of ready-made friends," Dusty said encouragingly. You could see he was an athlete himself. He had big shoulders and a sunburned nose that he rubbed a lot. There were bowling trophies on the windowsill and a memo pad with golf jokes on the desk.

"And I suck at it."

"Maybe we can change that."

"Really suck."

My mother was looking at me, her eyes narrow, and her earrings swinging. "I think it's a wonderful idea." The words came out without her hardly opening her mouth. "We're so grateful to you, Dusty, for suggesting it."

So I was paroled to the Tigers. I was released into my mother's custody, and she wouldn't let me bike home by myself, and she was feeling bad about Michael's spoiled evening. So she hissed me into Michael's car, apologizing the whole time to him. She suggested that we could maybe all go to the miniature golf course together. Michael agreed, but it wasn't his idea, and he and my mom were still dressed for a first impression.

I couldn't have been more miserable. I was hoping hard that Michael would turn out to be a jerk so that I would only have ruined the date, and not the rest of my mother's life. I hated him the minute I saw him, but you can't go by that. I could pretty much be counted on to hate every guy my mom went out with. This was easy since they were all jerks.

My mom was so mad at me that she couldn't miss. By the time we got to the fourth hole she was already three strokes under par. The fourth hole was the castle.

"I still don't get what not having a father has to do with shoplifting." There was a perfect little thwock sound when she hit the ball. She was clicking along on her two-inch heels and she *owned* this golf course.

Michael had been holding his tongue, but this was about the eighth time she'd said this. "It's not my business," he offered.

"But . . ."

Michael banked the ball off the side of the castle door and it rolled all the way back to his feet. "I just don't think his father would be letting him off so easy."

"What does that mean?"

"It means, here he is. Two hours ago the police picked him up for shoplifting. Is he being punished? No. You take him out for a game of miniature golf."

"Oh, he's not having a good time," my mom said. She turned to me. "Are you?"

"No, ma'am," I assured her.

"He stole something. If that'd been me, my father would have made real sure it never happened again," Michael said. "With his belt he would have made sure." Another ball missed the opening by inches.

"I have raised this kid all by myself for eleven years," my mother said. She was below us now, on the second half of the hole, sinking her putt. "I've done a great job. This is a great kid."

I saw the glimmer of a chance. "Don't make me play baseball, Mom." I put my heart into my voice.

"You. Don't. Even. Speak. to me," she answered.

By the time we got to the sixteenth hole, the anthill, we were really not getting along. "*Playboy!*" My mother was so far ahead there was no way for her to lose now. She'd forgotten about the dressed-up mousse in her hair, hair snot, she calls this. Sometime around hole seven she'd run her hand through it. Now it was sticking up in odd tufts. Of course, neither Michael nor I could tell her this even if we'd wanted to. She sank another ball. "I picketed the campus bookstore for carrying *Playboy*. Did you remember that, Nathan?"

I was hitting my balls too softly. I couldn't get them over the lip of the hole. Michael was hitting his balls too hard. They bounced into the hole and out again. He'd put his hair behind his ears, but it wouldn't stay there.

"There, you see . . ." Michael said.

"What?"

"Not that it's my business."

"Go ahead." My mom's voice was a wonder of nasty politeness. "Don't hold back."

"I just think a desire to look at *Playboy* magazine is pretty natural at his age. I think his father would understand that."

"I think *Playboy* promotes a degraded view of women. I think it's about power, not about sex. And I think Nathan knows how I feel."

Michael lined up his ball. He looked at the anthill, back down at his ball, looked at the anthill again. He took a little practice swing. "At a certain age, boys start to see breasts everywhere they look." He hit the ball too hard. "It's no big deal."

"I think that's six strokes," my mother said. "That would be your limit." She was snarling at him, her hair poking out of her head like pinfeathers.

His ears turned red. He snarled back. "It's not a real game."

"I think I've had six strokes, too," I said.

My mother retrieved her ball from the hole. "Don't *you* even speak to me."

• • •

Michael dropped us at home and we never saw him again. In my mind he lives forever, talking about breasts and taking that sad practice swing in his Star Trek tie. Because it was already midseason it took most of the next week to get me added to the Tigers' roster. Dusty let my mom know he was probably the only coach in town who could've accomplished it. His own son was the Tigers' top pitcher, a pleasant, pug-nosed kid named Ryan. Jeremy Campbell played third base.

My first game came on a Thursday night. So far I'd done nothing but strike out in practice and let ground balls go through my legs. While I was getting into my uniform my mom tossed a bag onto my bed. "What's this?" I asked. I opened it up. I was looking at something like a small white surgical mask, only rigid and with holes in it.

"Little something your coach said you might need," my mother told me.

"What is it?"

"An athletic cup."

"A *what?*"

"You wear it for protection."

I was starting to get it. What I was getting was horrifying. "I'm going to be hit in the balls? Is that what you're telling me?"

"Of course not."

"Then why am I wearing this?"

"So you don't have to worry even for a minute about it." Which of course I wasn't until this cup appeared. "I can show you how to wear it," my mom said. "On my hand."

"No!" I slammed the door. I couldn't get it comfortable, and I didn't know if this was because I wasn't wearing it right, or because it was just uncomfortable. In a million years I wouldn't ask my mother. I took it off and stowed it under the mattress.

Victor drove us to the game since we still didn't have a car. "It looks to me like your distributor got a bit wet," the mechanic had told my mom. "We could just dry it out, if that was all it was. But it looks to me like somebody just kept trying to start it and trying to start it until the starter burned out. Now your starter is shot and you're going to need a new battery too since it looks to me as if somebody tried to charge up the battery and thought they could just attach those jumper cables any which way. I wish you'd called us first thing when we could just have dried it out." He'd made my mom so mad she told him not to touch the car, but he'd let her leave it anyway, since we all knew she'd have to back down eventually.

So Victor drove us, and I tried to appeal to him. No way, I thought, could he have played baseball any better than I did. But he betrayed me, he was a scrappy little player, or so he chose to pretend. I've never yet met a grown man who'll admit he couldn't play ball. And then he added a second betrayal. "You watch too much television, Nathan." He had his arm stretched out comfortably across the seat back, driving with one hand. Nothing on his conscience at all. "This'll be good for you."

Tamara met us, since they all insisted on being in the stands for my debut. Because I was on the bench, I was practically sitting with them. I could hear them having a good time behind me, heading for the snack bar every couple of minutes, and I could have been having a good time too, except that I knew I had to go on the field eventually. Everyone plays, those were the stupid rules.

Ryan took the mound. A guy from the college was umping, a big, good-looking, long-armed cowboy of a guy named Chad. I heard my mom telling Tamara and Victor she thought he was cute and I was suddenly afraid she was going to like Little League way too much. Ryan warmed up and then the first batter stepped into the box. Ryan threw. "Strike!" Chad said.

"Good call, blue," my mother told him from the stands.

The other coach, a man with a red face, gray hair, and his ears sticking out on the outside of his baseball cap, called for a time-out. He spoke with Chad. "They're using an ineligible pitcher," he said. "We're filing a protest."

"You can talk to me," Dusty told him. "I'm right here. What the hell do you mean?"

"You pitched him Monday. All game. You can't use him again for four days."

Dusty counted on his fingers. "Monday, Tuesday, Wednesday, Thursday."

"You can't count Monday. You pitched him Monday."

"Did he pitch Monday?" Chad asked.

"Yes," Dusty said.

"Oh, you bet he did." The other coached pushed his hat back from his puffy, red face. "Thought I wouldn't notice?"

"I thought it was four days."

"Game goes to the Senators," Chad said.

"Wait. I'll pitch someone else," Dusty offered. "It was an honest mistake. Come on, he's only thrown a single pitch. The kids are all here to play. We'll start over."

"Not a chance." The other coach told the Senators to line up. "Shake their hands," he told them. "Give the Tigers a cheer. Let's show a little sportsmanship."

Back in the stands I could hear Victor saying how much better Little League would be if the kids made up the rules and didn't tell them to the parents. Whenever the parents started to figure them out, Victor suggested, the kids could change them.

But I thought this had worked out perfectly. Chad was already picking up the bases. My mom called to him that he umped one hell of a game. "Don't give me such a hard time, lady," he said, but he was all smiling when he said it; he came over to talk to her. Dusty took the team out for ice cream. There was a white owl in the air and a cloud of moths around the streetlights. A breeze came in from the almond orchards. I was one happy ballplayer.

Of course they wouldn't all be like that. Sooner or later I could see I was going to be out in right field with the ball headed for my uncupped crotch, the game on the line, and Jeremy Campbell watching me from third.

• • •

On Friday my mother called and told the garage to go ahead and fix the car. This was a defeat and she took it as such. I didn't have another game until Monday, but I did have practice on Friday so I was not as happy as I could have been either. The practice field was on the way home from the garage so Mom drove by later after she'd picked up the car. The weather was hot and the team was just assembling. She stopped for a moment to watch and then the car wouldn't start. "Jesus Christ!" she said. She banged the horn once in frustration; it gave a startled caw.

Jeremy came biking in beside her. He started to pedal past, then swung around. "Pop the hood," he told her.

"I picked this car up from the garage about two minutes ago. I won't even tell you what I just paid that crook."

Jeremy lifted the hood. "Your ground strap came off." He did something I couldn't see; when my mom turned the key, it started right up.

"What a *wonderful* boy," she said to me. To him, "You're a wonderful boy."

"Forget it." Jeremy was all gracious modesty.

She took off then, engine churning like butter, and we'd just barely started passing the ball around when

Dusty got called away on a 911. The assistant coach hadn't arrived yet, so Dusty told us all to go straight on home again. After Dusty left, Jeremy chased me into Putah Creek Park, where my bicycle skidded out from under me when I tried to make a fast, evasive turn. He threw my bike down into the creek gully. He left me lying on the ground, hating myself for being afraid to even stand up, thinking of ways I could kill him. I could run him through with a magic sword. I could hang him from a meathook. I could smother him with his own athletic cup. If I bashed his skull with a baseball bat, no one would ever suspect it was me.

The bank of the creek was steep. I slid all the way down it. Then I slipped in the mud trying to get myself and the bicycle out again. The creek was already covered with summer slime and I got slick, green, fish-smelling streaks of it on my pants. My shoes were ruined. The front wheel of the bike was bent and I had to carry it home, rolling it on the back tire.

This was a long, hard, hot walk. I loved my bicycle, but there were many, many moments when I considered just walking off and leaving it. I'd hit my knees and my hands on the pavement when I fell, and my injuries stung and throbbed while I was walking. I told my mother I'd fallen off the bike, which was certainly true, and she bought it, even though I'd never fallen off my bike before, and certainly not into the creek.

Tamara was singing at Cafe Roma that evening and my mother had mentioned it to Chad, so she was thinking he might show. It had her distracted and she didn't make the fuss over my injuries that I expected. She was busy borrowing clothes from Tamara and moussing up her hair. This was a good thing, I thought, fewer questions to deal with and it probably meant I was growing up. But the lack of attention made me even more miserable than I already was. It would have all been worthwhile if my injuries had kept me out of Monday's game, but they didn't.

When everyone had left the house I took a hammer to the athletic cup. I meant to prove the cup wasn't up to much, but I found out otherwise. The blows bounced off it without leaving a mark. To make sure the hammer wasn't defective I tested it on the floor in my room. I left a ding like a crescent in the linoleum inside my closet. I smashed up a bunch of old crayons and put a hole in the bedroom wall behind the bed. I took an apple I hadn't eaten at lunch outside and crushed it like an egg. I was more and more impressed with the cup. I just needed a whole suit of the stuff.

This was all about the same time Boston third baseman Wade Boggs went on national TV and told the world he was addicted to sex.

• • •

We had a game Monday against the Royals and, like a nightmare, suddenly, there we were, down by one run, two outs, sixth and final inning, with Bjorn Benson on first base and me at bat. So far I'd only connected with the ball once and that was a feeble foul. Jeremy came out to the box to give me a little pep talk. "This used to be a good team before you joined," he said. "But you suck. If you cost us this game you'll pay in ways you can't even imagine, faggot." He smelled of cigarettes, though no one in my town smoked; it was like a town ordinance. Jeremy spit into the dust beside my cleats. I turned to look at the stands and I saw my mother watching us.

Dusty came and took the bat out of my hand. He went to the umpire, who wasn't Chad. "Ryan batting for Nathan," he said. He sent me back to the bench. It took Ryan seven pitches to strike out, which is surely four more pitches than it would have taken me.

Our car wasn't working again and Victor had dropped us off, but he couldn't stay for the whole game, so my mom asked Dusty's wife, Linda, a pretty woman who wore lipstick even to the ballpark, for a ride home.

When we got in the car we were all quiet for a while. Dusty finally spoke. "You played a good game, Nathan. You too, Ryan."

Linda agreed. "It was a good game. Nothing to be ashamed of."

"Usually you can hit off Alex," Dusty said to Ryan. "I wonder what happened tonight."

"He didn't get to bed until late," Linda suggested. "Were you tired, honey?"

"I don't think Alex was pitching as fast as he usually does. I thought he was tiring. I thought you'd hit off him."

"That was a lot of pressure, putting him in then," Linda observed. "But usually he would have gotten a hit. Were you tired, honey?"

"One more pitch, we would have had him, right, Tigers?"

Ryan looked out the window and didn't say much. There was a song on the radio, "Believe It or Not," and his lips were moving as if he was singing along but I couldn't hear him.

They let us off and we went inside. Like Ryan, my mom had been quiet the whole way home. I went to clean up and then she called me into the kitchen. "Couple of things," she said. "First of all, you're scared of that boy. The one who fixed our car. Why?"

"Because he's scary?" I offered. "Because he's a huge, mean, cretinous freak who hates me?" I was relieved, but mortified that she knew. I was also surprised. It was too much to feel all at once. I made things worse by starting to cry, loudly, and with my shoulders shaking.

My mom put her arms around me and held me until I stopped. "I love you," she said. She kissed the top of my head.

"I love you, too."

"I loved you first." Her arms tightened on me. "So there's a rumor on the street that you don't want to play baseball anymore."

I pushed away to look at her face. She stuck out her tongue and crossed her eyes.

"You mean it?" I asked. "I can quit?"

"I'll call Dusty tonight and tell him he's short one little Tiger."

It turned out to be a little more complicated. My mom called Dusty, but Dusty said he needed to see me, said he needed to hear it from me. He'd made representations to Mr. Bertilucci, he reminded us. He didn't want those to have been false representations. He thought we owed it to him to listen to what he had to say. He asked us to come to the house.

My mom agreed. By now we had the car back again. My mother drove and on the way over she warned me about the good cop/bad cop routine she thought Dusty and Linda might be planning to pull. She promised she wouldn't leave me alone with Dusty and she was as good as her word even when Linda tried to entice her outside to show her where the new deck was going to go. Ryan had obviously made himself scarce.

We sat in the living room, which was done country style, white ruffles and blue-and-white checks. Someone, I'm guessing Linda, collected ceramic ducks. She stood at the kitchen door smiling nervously at us. The TV was on in the background, the local news with the affable local anchor. Dusty muted her to talk to me. "You haven't really given the team or yourself a chance," Dusty said. His face had a ruddy, healthy glow.

"I just don't like baseball."

"You don't like it because you think you're no good at it. Give yourself time to get better." He turned to my mother. "You shouldn't let him give up on himself."

"He's not giving up on himself. He's being himself."

"He was improving every game," Linda said.

"He never wanted to play. I made him."

Dusty leaned forward. "And I remember why you made him. You want that to happen again?"

"That's a separate issue."

"I don't think so," Dusty turned to me again. "Don't let yourself become one of the quitters, Nathan. Don't walk out on your team. The values you learn on the playing field, those are the values that make you a success in everything you do later in life."

"I never played on a team," my mom observed. "How ever do I manage to get through the day?"

It was a snotty comment. Really, she was the one who started it. Dusty was the one to go for the throat. "I'm sure his father wouldn't want him taught to be a quitter."

There was a long, slow, loud silence in the room. Then my mom was talking without moving her mouth again. "His father is none of your damn business."

"Would anyone like a cup of coffee?" Linda asked. Her sandals tapped anxiously as she started into the kitchen, then came back out again. "I made brownies! I hope everyone likes them with nuts!"

Neither my mom nor Dusty showed any sign of hearing her. Neither would take their eyes off the other. "He didn't quit on you, Dusty," my mom said. "You quit on him."

"What does that mean?"

"It was his turn to bat."

"That was okay with me," I pointed out. "I was really happy with that."

"That was a team decision," Dusty said. "That's just what I'm talking about. If you'd ever played on a team you wouldn't be questioning that decision."

My mother stood, taking me by the hand. "You run your team. Let me raise my kid," she said. And we left the house and one of us left it hopping mad. "On the planet Zandoor," she told me, "Little League is just for adults. Dusty wouldn't qualify. Of course it's not like Little League here. You try to design a glove that fits on a Zandoorian."

The other one of us was so happy he was floating. When we got home Victor, Tamara, and Chad were sitting together on our porch. "I'm not a baseball player anymore," I told them. I couldn't stop grinning about it.

"Way to go, champ," Tamara said. She put her arms around me. Her body was much softer than my mom's and her black hair fell over my face so I smelled her coconut shampoo. It was a perfect moment. I remember everything about it.

"What do you think of that?" my mom asked Chad. Through the curtain of Tamara's hair I watched him shrug. "If he doesn't like to play, why should he play?"

They were staring at each other. I thought he was a little young for her, besides being a fat jerk, but no one was asking me. "Saturday night," she told him, "there's a

Take Back the Night march downtown. Victor, Tamara, and I are going. Do you want to come?"

Chad looked at Victor. "This is a test, isn't it?" he asked.

"You already passed the test," my mother said.

The next day she spotted Jeremy while she was dropping me at school She waved him over and he actually came. "I'm so glad to see you," she told him. "I didn't thank you properly for helping with the car the other day. You were great. Where did you learn to do that?"

"My dad," Jeremy said.

"I'm going to call him up and thank him, too. Tell him what a great kid he has. And you should come to dinner. I owe you that much. Honestly, you'd be doing me a favor. I'm thinking of buying a new car, but I need someone knowledgeable advising me." She was laying it on so thick the air was hard to breathe.

Jeremy suggested a Mustang convertible, or maybe a Trans Am. He was walking away before she'd turn and see the look I was giving her. "That's wonderful," I said. "Jeremy Campbell is coming to dinner. That's a dream come true." I gathered up my homework, slammed the car door, stormed off. Then I came back. "And it won't work," I told her. "You don't know him like I do."

"Maybe not," my mom said. "But it's hard to dislike someone you've been good to, someone who's depending on you. It's an old women's trick. I think it's worth a try."

Let me just take a moment here to note that it did not work. Jeremy Campbell didn't even show up for the dinner my mom cooked specially for him. He did ease off for a bit until whatever it was about me that provoked him provoked him again. Not a thing worked with Jeremy until Mr. Campbell was laid off and the whole Campbell family finally had to move three states east. The last time I saw him was June of 1991. He was sitting on top of me, pinning my shoulders down with his knees, stuffing dried leaves into my mouth. He had an unhappy look on his face as if he didn't like it any more than I did, and that pissed me off more than anything.

Then he turned his head slightly and a beam of pure light came streaming through his ears, lighting them up, turning them into two bright red fungi at the sides of his head. It helped a little that he looked ridiculous, even though I was the only one in the right position to see. It's the picture I keep in my heart.

• • •

So that's the way it really was and don't let my mother tell you differently. Saturday turned out to be the night I won at *The Legend of Zelda*. I was alone in the house at the time. Mom and Tamara were off at their rally, marching down Second Street, carrying signs. The Playboy Bunny logo in a red circle with a red slash across its face. On my computer the theme played and the princess kissed the hero, again and again. These words appeared on the screen: *You have destroyed Ganon. Peace has returned to the country of Hyrule.*

And then the words vanished and were replaced with another message. *Do you wish to play again?*

What I wished was that I had *The Adventure of Link.* But before I could get bitter, the phone rang. "This is really embarrassing," my mom said. "There was a little trouble at the demonstration. We've been arrested."

"Arrested for what?" I asked.

"Assault. Mayhem. Crimes of a violent nature. None of the charges will stick. We were attacked by a group of nazi frat boys and I did nothing but defend my-self. You know me. Only thing is, Dusty is in no mood to cut me any slack. I don't think I'm getting out tonight. What a vindictive bastard he's turned out to be!"

"Are you all right?"

"Oh, yeah. Hardly a scratch." There was a lot of noise in the background. I could just make out Tamara, she was singing that Merle Haggard song "Mama Tried." "There's a whole bunch of us here," my mother said. "It's the crime of the century. I might get my picture in the paper. Anyway, Victor wasn't arrested. You know Victor. So he's on his way to stay with you tonight. I just wanted you to hear from me yourself."

I didn't like to think of her spending the night in jail, even if it did sound like a slumber party over there. I could already hear Victor's car pulling up out front. I was glad he was staying; I wouldn't have liked to be alone all night. Sometime in the dark I'd have started thinking about nuns with hooks for hands. Now I could see him through the window and he was carrying a pizza. Good on Victor! "Just as long as you're all right," I told her.

"I must say you're being awfully nice about this," my mother said.

BIBLIOGRAPHY

PARTIAL LIST OF PUBLICATIONS

Novels

We Are All Completely Beside Ourselves. New York: G.P. Putnam's Sons, 2013.

Wit's End. New York: G.P. Putnam's Sons, 2008.

The Jane Austen Book Club. New York: Putnam, 2004; subsequently published in 27 languages.

Sister Noon. New York: Putnam, 2001.

The Sweetheart Season: A Novel. New York: Henry Holt, 1996

Sarah Canary. New York: Henry Holt, 1991

Stories

What I Didn't See, and Other Stories. Easthampton, MA: Small Beer Press, 2010.

Black Glass: Short Fictions. New York: Henry Holt, 1998.

Letters from Home: Stories, by Pat Cadigan, Karen Joy Fowler, and Pat Murphy. London: Women's Press, 1991.

Artificial Things. New York: Bantam Books, 1986.

Künstliche Dinge. München: Heyne Verlag, 1991.

Peripheral Vision. Eugene, OR: Pulphouse, 1990.

ABOUT THE AUTHOR

KAREN JOY FOWLER ATTENDED Berkeley during the tumultuous 1960s, earning a degree in political science. She took up writing at thirty after her youngest child started first grade. Her mainstream novels and her science fiction short stories are known for their wry wit, uncompromising humanism, and radical "take" on feminist and other social issues.

The author of six novels and three short story collections, she is also a cofounder of the James Tiptree Jr. Memorial Award and current president of the Clarion Foundation, which exists to support the annual Clarion Writing Workshop at University of California, San Diego.

Her most famous novel is *The Jane Austen Book Club*, and her most recent novel is *We Are All Completely Beside Ourselves*, published by Putnam in 2013.

She lives with her husband in Santa Cruz, where they go to sleep each night to the dulcet tones of barking sea lions.

PM PRESS
OUTSPOKEN AUTHORS

Surfing the Gnarl
Rudy Rucker
128 Pages
$12.00

The original "Mad Professor" of Cyberpunk, Rudy Rucker (along with fellow outlaws William Gibson and Bruce Sterling) transformed modern science fiction, tethering the "gnarly" speculations of quantum physics to the noir sensibilities of a skeptical and disenchanted generation. In acclaimed novels like *Wetware* and *The Hacker and the Ant* he mapped a neotopian future that belongs not to sober scientists but to drug-addled, sex-crazed youth. And won legions of fans doing it.

In his outrageous new story "The Men in the Back Room at the Country Club," Dr. Rucker infiltrates fundamentalist Virginia to witness the apocalyptic clash between Bible-thumpers and Saucer Demons at a country club barbecue. He shoots erotica into orbit with "Rapture in Space" to explore the future of foreplay in freefall. In his gonzo nonfiction masterpiece "Surfing the Gnarl," he documents the role of the Transreal in transforming both the personal and the political, distinguishes with mathematical precision between "high gnarl" and "low gnarl" in literature and life, and argues for remaking popular culture as a revolutionary project.

And Featuring: PM's exclusive Outspoken Interview, in which the author explains Infinity, deconstructs his own outrageous film career, answers one *Jeopardy* question, and (finally!) reveals the truth about Time. All under oath.

PM PRESS
OUTSPOKEN AUTHORS

Report from Planet Midnight
Nalo Hopkinson
128 Pages
$12.00

Nalo Hopkinson has been busily (and wonderfully) "subverting the genre" since her first novel, *Brown Girl in the Ring*, won a Locus Award for SF and Fantasy in 1999. Since then she has acquired a prestigious World Fantasy Award, a legion of adventurous and aware fans, a reputation for intellect seasoned with humor, and a place of honor in the short list of SF writers who are tearing down the walls of category and transporting readers to previously unimagined planets and realms.

Never one to hold her tongue, Hopkinson takes on sexism and racism in publishing in "Report from Planet Midnight," a historic and controversial presentation to her colleagues and fans.

Plus...

"Message in a Bottle," a radical new twist on the time travel tale that demolishes the sentimental myth of childhood innocence; and "Shift," a tempestuous erotic adventure in which Caliban gets the girl. Or does he?

And Featuring: our Outspoken Interview, an intimate one-on-one that delivers a wealth of insight, outrage, irreverence, and top-secret Caribbean spells.

"Rapidly emerging as the William Gibson of his generation"
—ENTERTAINMENT WEEKLY

PM PRESS
OUTSPOKEN AUTHORS

The Great Big Beautiful Tomorrow
Cory Doctorow
144 Pages
$12.00

Cory Doctorow burst on the SF scene in 2000 like a rocket, inspiring awe in readers (and envy in other writers) with his bestselling novels and stories, which he insisted on giving away via Creative Commons. Meanwhile, as coeditor of the wildly popular blog Boing Boing, he became the radical new voice of the Web, boldly arguing for internet freedom from corporate control.

Doctorow's activism and artistry are both on display in this Outspoken Author edition. The crown jewel is his novella, *The Great Big Beautiful Tomorrow*, the high-velocity adventures of a transhuman teenager in a toxic post-Disney dystopia, battling wireheads and wumpuses (and having fun doing it!) until he meets the "meat girl" of his dreams, and is forced to choose between immortality and sex.

Plus...

A live transcription of Cory's historic address to the 2010 World SF Convention, "Creativity vs. Copyright," dramatically presenting his controversial case for open-source in both information and art.

Also included is an international Outspoken Interview (Skyped from England, Canada, and the U.S.) in which Doctorow reveals the surprising sources of his genius.

PM PRESS
OUTSPOKEN AUTHORS

The Wild Girls
Ursula K. Le Guin
112 Pages
$12.00

Ursula K. Le Guin is the one modern science fiction author who truly needs no introduction. In the forty years since *The Left Hand of Darkness*, her works have changed not only the face but the tone and the agenda of SF, introducing themes of gender, race, socialism, and anarchism, all the while thrilling readers with trips to strange (and strangely familiar) new worlds. She is our exemplar of what fantastic literature can and should be about.

Her Nebula winner *The Wild Girls*, newly revised and presented here in book form for the first time, tells of two captive "dirt children" in a society of sword and silk, whose determination to enter "that possible even when unattainable space in which there is room for justice" leads to a violent and loving end.

Plus...

Le Guin's scandalous and scorching *Harper's* essay, "Staying Awake While We Read," (also collected here for the first time) which demolishes the pretensions of corporate publishing and the basic assumptions of capitalism as well. And of course our Outspoken Interview, which promises to reveal the hidden dimensions of America's best-known SF author. And delivers.

A writer of powerful imagination and emotion ...
—URSULA K. LEGUIN

PM PRESS
OUTSPOKEN AUTHORS

Mammoths of the Great Plains
Eleanor Arnason
152 Pages
$12.00

When President Thomas Jefferson sent Lewis and Clark to explore the West, he told them to look especially for mammoths. Jefferson had seen bones and tusks of the great beasts in Virginia, and he suspected—he hoped!—that they might still roam the Great Plains. In Eleanor Arnason's imaginative alternate history, they do: shaggy herds thunder over the grasslands, living symbols of the oncoming struggle between the Native peoples and the European invaders. And in an unforgettable saga that soars from the badlands of the Dakotas to the icy wastes of Siberia, from the Russian Revolution to the AIM protests of the 1960s, Arnason tells of a modern woman's struggle to use the weapons of DNA science to fulfill the ancient promises of her Lakota heritage.

Plus...

"Writing SF During World War III," and an Outspoken Interview that takes you straight into the heart and mind of one of today's edgiest and most uncompromising speculative authors.

> "Eleanor Arnason nudges both human and natural history around so gently in this tale that you hardly know you're not in the world-as-we-know-it until you're quite at home in a North Dakota where you've never been before, listening to your grandmother tell you the world."
> —Ursula K. Le Guin

FRIENDS OF

These are indisputably momentous times—the financial system is melting down globally and the Empire is stumbling. Now more than ever there is a vital need for radical ideas.

In the six years since its founding—and on a mere shoestring—PM Press has risen to the formidable challenge of publishing and distributing knowledge and entertainment for the struggles ahead. With over 250 releases to date, we have published an impressive and stimulating array of literature, art, music, politics, and culture. Using every available medium, we've succeeded in connecting those hungry for ideas and information to those putting them into practice.

Friends of PM allows you to directly help impact, amplify, and revitalize the discourse and actions of radical writers, filmmakers, and artists. It provides us with a stable foundation from which we can build upon our early successes and provides a much-needed subsidy for the materials that can't necessarily pay their own way. You can help make that happen—and receive every new title automatically delivered to your door once a month—by joining as a Friend of PM Press. And, we'll throw in a free T-Shirt when you sign up.

Here are your options:
- $30 a month: Get all books and pamphlets plus 50% discount on all webstore purchases
- $40 a month: Get all PM Press releases (including CDs and DVDs) plus 50% discount on all webstore purchases
- $100 a month: Superstar—Everything plus PM merchandise, free downloads, and 50% discount on all webstore purchases

For those who can't afford $30 or more a month, we're introducing Sustainer Rates at $15, $10, and $5. Sustainers get a free PM Press T-shirt and a 50% discount on all purchases from our website.

Your Visa or Mastercard will be billed once a month, until you tell us to stop. Or until our efforts succeed in bringing the revolution around. Or the financial meltdown of Capital makes plastic redundant. Whichever comes first.

PM Press was founded at the end of 2007 by a small collection of folks with decades of publishing, media, and organizing experience. PM Press co-conspirators have published and distributed hundreds of books, pamphlets, CDs, and DVDs. Members of PM have founded enduring book fairs, spearheaded victorious tenant organizing campaigns, and worked closely with bookstores, academic conferences, and even rock bands to deliver political and challenging ideas to all walks of life. We're old enough to know what we're doing and young enough to know what's at stake.

We seek to create radical and stimulating fiction and non-fiction books, pamphlets, T-shirts, visual and audio materials to entertain, educate and inspire you. We aim to distribute these through every available channel with every available technology—whether that means you are seeing anarchist classics at our bookfair stalls; reading our latest vegan cookbook at the café; downloading geeky fiction e-books; or digging new music and timely videos from our website.

PM Press is always on the lookout for talented and skilled volunteers, artists, activists and writers to work with. If you have a great idea for a project or can contribute in some way, please get in touch.

PM Press
PO Box 23912
Oakland CA 94623
510-658-3906
www.pmpress.org